Love Fumbles:

A High School Romance Novel about a Quarterback, Race, and Relationships in 1960's Louisiana

By Regina Smith

For Ken and Lillie

Prologue

With his fork, thirteen-year-old Paul Boudreaux took a tiny bite from his steak. Timidly, he chewed until it was nothing more than mash in his mouth. Dinner in the dining room was a meager shell of what it had been in the past. Instead of the regular conversations, things were silent and awkward. The empty chair across from him was no longer filled. In fact, all the other chairs at the table were unoccupied, except the one at the head of the table. In that chair sat Paul's grandfather, Abraham Boudreaux, a bitter, incensed, and leery man. He cut deeply into his steak. His lips were pointed downward with the utmost revulsion. His penetrating grey eyes squinted at the dish, as if absorbed by an obnoxious thought. Abraham's well-groomed grey hair tilted forward mirroring his exasperations. His plain white shirt was neatly buttoned, and his solid dark grey pants were tailor made. The elderly man, who was in his late seventies, avoided glancing at the seat directly across from Paul, reminding young Paul of his mother's words from years ago.

"Never EVER upset your grandfather," Paul's mother had always warned him. *"He is a very powerful man and looks to you as his favorite grandson, but even his loyalty can be fleeting if he changes his mind about you."*

Since then, Paul began doing whatever it took to be the best in school and sports, even agreeing to do additional tasks at the family store called Sal's Country Store that had been passed down through the generations, losing himself within their high expectations of him being the ideal child. Everyone had to adore him, and he had to do whatever it took to win people over, surpassing even his grandfather's expectations of the youth. Without Abraham's favor, Paul could be scum like the rest, who were no longer welcomed.

Knock! Knock!

Abraham's head jerked towards the door. He balled his fists, tightly gripping the utensils. He slammed both fists against the table. Startled, Paul leapt back in his chair. Now facing him, Abraham directed for the boy to answer the door. Promptly, Paul pushed his chair back and left the dinner table. He walked to the front door where two familiar men were standing outside. Without a word, both men entered the home. They both were part of The Family, a racist organization led by Abraham with Klan ties within the small town of Wood Oak, Louisiana. One man worked for Abraham and the other was Paul's cousin, Wally Boudreaux, a young man who had just turned twenty-years-old days ago.

Removing his hat, the first man, stopped at the entrance of the dining room. He was sweating heavily and rubbing the back of his neck. Wally stood a yard behind the man and Paul returned to his place at the table.

"You dare to disturb my dinner with my grandson?" Abraham demanded, cutting into his steak.

"I-it's the Wilkerson family," the man said. "They came up short this month. Edward was doing some home repairs and had an accident. He didn't have any insurance and hasn't been able to do his regular duties at his job. His boss told him that he could still keep his job, but they cannot pay him until he is healed and goes back to work. Edward has been unable to work the last few weeks. His family is also behind on their bills."

Unconcerned, Abraham bit into his steak.

"They have nothing, sir, and have been extremely loyal within The Family," the man continued. "This is the first time they have been unable to pay their dues and are in a desperate situation, being a family of thirteen."

Abraham took a sip of water from his cup and turned to his grandson, Paul.

"Since Paul will be handling matters as my heir, he will decide," the old man said.

Eyes soon descended upon Paul, who had witnessed his grandfather determine the fates of many people within The Family. Often, people went to Abraham seeking financial assistance, in return for favors and agreed upon payments. This time, a first for Paul, would be his initial 'business transaction.' He was thirteen and now the fate of a desperate family was in his hands. The Wilkerson family had a son Paul's age named Henry. Henry had always been cordial to him, despite his animosity for everyone else outside of his own family. The two had even formed a close friendship, regardless of their distinct social and financial positions within the community.

"I am going to help them," Paul said. "Give them an extension on their dues because of their circumstances. Our family store and some other small businesses around town can help sell some goods for Mrs. Wilkerson since she is a good cook, and the family could use the funds. We can also offer a loan at a five percent interest rate, should they need it."

"Five percent is hardly a profit," Abraham muttered. "But, given that I allowed you to decide, I will grant it." He faced the man. "Give our notices to the Wilkerson family and extend their time for three months. My grandson has been more than generous; should they fail to pay their dues next time, I will more than quadruple it."

The man went away, leaving Wally standing at the doorway to the dining room. Instantaneously, Abraham's eyes bulged at the sheer sight of his other grandson. His face turned almost a beet red as a noticeable vein twitched on his neck.

"You got guts coming back here," Abraham snapped, pointing his knife at Wally. "You *thief*! You dared to steal from *me*, of all people."

Wally's face was soddened in tears and distraught. There had been a time when he, too, was in Abraham's good graces, like Paul. There had been many dinners, decisions, and other matters that the two once shared as protégé and mentor, but that was now a thing of the past. Wally was no longer authorized to make any financial judgments or handle any other decisions that were once given to him by his grandfather.

"I was going to give it back," Wally wailed from the door entrance, not daring to go any further. "I had no choice! You knew that I needed the money to get the house—."

"You're blaming me because you couldn't manage your own finances to get a home on your own?" Abraham interrupted.

"I had to leave," Wally wept. "I can't stand living with Pop. It's unbearable! He beats mom every day, and I can't take it anymore!"

"He should have been beating you too, you damn thief," Abraham said.

"I had nowhere else to go. You're always saying that everyone is welcomed here; yet you turned me away and forced me to live with them. How come Paul could stay here with you and I couldn't? I can make greater profits for you at the store than he can! Look at him! He's a little kid and is always feeling sorry for people!"

Abraham's face relaxed. The grip to his utensils softened. He smirked and leaned back into his chair. The old man roared with laughter that resonated throughout the room with the eyes of both grandsons upon him. The old man beckoned for Wally to come closer to him. Calmer, Wally approached Abraham, who nodded for Wally to sit at his usual seat at the table, across from Paul.

"I will settle this matter," Abraham declared to both grandsons. "Wally, you will be moving back into Harry's home and the house you are living in now will be placed back on the market. Any money you've gotten from me will be given to Paul, along with any hopes of you ever becoming my heir."

Wally froze.

"You say that you can make great profits," Abraham continued. "Show me! You will continue to work at Sal's until you can prove to me that you can make an enormous profit on your own by starting at the very bottom, saving your own money. You dare to bad mouth your uncle who adopted you as his own son? *To me*? You will continue to eat from *his* table, living as *he* sees fit, as a beggar in his house until you realize how grateful you should be to him."

"But--."

"Pipe down! You all are nothing but an embarrassment to me, except for Paul. He is well liked and has an exceptional reputation, as his father had. The rest of you deserve nothing. I gave you all money, places to live, power...everything! How do you pay me back? Stealing from me, fighting amongst each other in public, making horrible business deals behind my back, the list goes on! Except for Paul, the rest of you are out of my will! Get out of my house!"

Livid, Wally stormed out of the home.

Chapter 1

Boisterously, the school bell at Wood Oak High School chimed, drawing the attention to all on campus, beginning the start of the new school day in Wood Oak, Louisiana. Wood Oak was a town that had a disquieting past, as some would say, long before the year of 1969. The last only colored school, Freedmen's High School, burned to the ground days ago, leaving those students nowhere to go other than the predominantly white school, Wood Oak High School. Previously, there had been attempts to integrate the Negro students into Wood Oak High School, but several disagreeable families saw to it that those students were removed. There had been protests, harassments, and threats, forcing the removal of those students for their safety. Since then, no students from Freedmen's High School dared to enter Wood Oak High School and were deemed "dummies" within the Negro community for even having thoughts of ever going back. However, on this new school day, there would be another attempt in which several Negro students would once again be brought back into that same high school because there was no other high school to go to within their community.

The hallways were crowded with several white students engaging in their usual conversations of the most recent sporting events, one of which was a popular jock named Paul Boudreaux, who was now a seventeen-year-old senior. Wearing his white shirt, dark green and white letterman sweater, dark blue jeans, and leather shoes, Paul strolled down the corridor with the highest confidence. His profound laughter reverberated throughout the hallway, veering many heads his way, and bringing smiles to several students. His jet-black hair stood in the trendy pompadour-style and his arrogant smirk softened the hearts of many girls. His eyes were a mesmerizing, mysterious grey. Everything about him appeared perfect and by many standards set by the popular teens, Paul could be anything and do anything he wanted. He was the quarterback of the football team, the captain of the baseball team, and the best male dancer at the sock-hop events. He was number one and his handsome looks made him the ultimate hunk. Most of the school looked up to Paul and all eyes were on him, seeing what the next big thing would be, with *his* approval. Unfortunately, for him, he was part of the Boudreaux family and was the *only* one that had a positive reputation. The rest of his family were despised throughout the community by both whites and Negroes.

Bill Boudreaux, Paul's cousin, also attended the same high school as a seventeen-year-old senior. He shared the similar black hair and grey eyes, but everything else was the total opposite. Bill was overweight, had enlarged hands and feet, was shunned, and was detested throughout the school by everyone. His icy blue shirt mirrored the coldness of his heart, and his orange and red plaid pants reflected his intense, malevolent fury. Bill was often obscene and was prone to getting into many physical and verbal altercations with countless students, often knocking them unconscious with a single punch. Apart from his fighting skills, Bill had no other athletic competencies whatsoever and would be the first person to heavily criticize someone else's shortcomings. He was a bully and thrived on making the lives of others miserable. Kind words rarely escaped his lips and those that did were given to Paul's girlfriend, Nancy Perkins, a girl that Bill believed was stolen from him by Paul.

Nancy Perkins, also a seventeen-year-old senior, was the popular captain of the cheerleaders. She had been Paul's girlfriend since last school year. She had long, dark brown hair and dark blue eyes. She wore a dark green and white letterman sweater over her white shirt and solid green skirt with green knee-high socks over her oxford shoes. Often perceived as jovial, Nancy maintained an outwardly optimistic attitude while hiding her distaste for the unpopular students and their lack of fashion sense or smarts. Nancy had fallen in love with Paul since they both entered the high school together, but Paul was with another girl. Once the other girl had moved away unexpectantly, Nancy seized the opportunity to become Paul's new girl. Her focus had been him, often ignoring Bill's desperate attempts to gain her affections years prior.

Entering the classroom ahead of the others was Paul's best-friend, Henry Wilkerson. Henry was another seventeen-year-old athlete. He had red hair, blue eyes, and pale skin covered in freckles. He wore a letterman sweater, with a blue shirt, brown slacks, and leather shoes. Unlike his best-friend, Henry was often perceived as a "jerk", and was only liked for his capability to help the team win games, coming in second to Paul's impressive athleticism. Henry would do anything for Paul; the two friends had been close since elementary school and would often be seen together talking about the latest cars, sports, and girls.

Their math teacher was Mr. Thomas, a veteran teacher, in his late fifties, who had been teaching at the school for over twenty years. Barely making it into the classroom before the last bell ring, Mr. Thomas closed the door behind the popular students. The rest of the class laughed as the four teens sat down in their usual seats, before turning back to the front of the classroom where Mr. Thomas and two new students were standing.

Mr. Thomas cleared his throat and the class hushed as their eyes centered on *them*. There was a Negro female with golden, dark brown skin and eyes. Her black hair was in a short bouffant hairstyle. She was dressed in a solid dark brown sweater, a solid orange blouse, a plaid yellow and orange skirt, orange socks, and saddle shoes. The outfit was slightly faded, indicating that it must have been second hand. The girl's eyes were dead locked to the floor, exhibiting more discomfort by the second. Standing next to her was a Negro male with dark brown skin and eyes and a short black afro. He wore a faded yellow and brown plaid shirt with a pocket that had a pencil and pen in it, solid brown pants, brown socks, and faded tennis shoes. Additionally, he had big round glasses that triggered several students to chuckle at such an absurd appearance. His nervous face and stance also appeared to be one of discomfort, but he kept his head up, with his eyes staring into the far distance and away from the gazes and giggles of the other students.

"Class," Mr. Thomas announced, "we have two new students: Nell Jefferson and Martin Parker. They will be spending their last school year with us. Do your best to make them feel welcomed."

The class was dead silent, awkward, and unwelcoming. All desks were taken, except for the last two in the back of the classroom. One desk was missing the top and the other desk was tilting precariously to the left. Normally, those types of desks would have been removed from the classroom immediately, but today, they were not. Mr. Thomas instructed the two new students to take the last remaining seats as Bill snorted his disapproval. Martin took the desk with no top and Nell took the tilting seat, which began to lean towards the center. She grasped it by the top and used her foot to steady the desk. Turning his focus back to the task at hand, Mr. Thomas began to introduce the new math equations to the class on the chalkboard.

"Why they got to let those dumb monkeys into *our* class?" Bill whispered to Paul.

Paul shrugged his shoulders and took out a pencil and paper to take his notes. This being his senior year, Paul could care less about any new students. He needed to make sure that his grades were good enough to maintain his status as the quarterback on the football team. His football coach, Coach Anderson, had informed Paul that college scouts would be watching the team this year and he might have the chance to receive a scholarship into a good university. Paul did not care much for school, but he did like sports and any chance to be the best meant the most to him. However, if his grades weren't maintained, Coach Anderson wouldn't think twice about replacing him as the quarterback for one game and the last thing Paul wanted was for another teammate to outshine him, especially if scouts would be on the watch.

Mr. Thomas asked the class if there were any questions. A hand slowly lifted from the back of the classroom. The class paused and faced the bashful Negro girl in the back. Fretfully, she began to slightly tug at her sweater before responding.

"I'm sorry, sir," Nell said. "I don't understand."

Several students groaned, while others giggled. Bill tossed his head back.

"Why is *she* even in our class?" he groaned. "She is as dumb as rocks, fuckin' idiot."

Mr. Thomas silenced the class by raising his hand. He tipped his glasses slightly.

"Rudeness is not helping," he said. "I apologize for the class, Nell. It is okay to say that you do not understand. I will go over it again and we can try an alternative method to solve the equation."

"Great," Bill grumbled, "now the rest of us are going to be behind and dumbed down at this rate."

Pop! The class grew silent. *Pop!* Mr. Thomas and the rest of the class turned to the right of the classroom and at Nancy Perkins. She was in her own world, twirling parts of her hair with her fingers, and chewing gum. Her mouth opened and then a tiny piece of pink gum squeezed between her lips and grew in size. *Pop!* It burst between her lips. Nancy sucked the gum back inside her mouth, chewing the gum.

"Nancy," Mr. Thomas said.

"Yes, Mr. Thomas?" Nancy said, still writing her notes and oblivious of her blunder.

"Are you chewing gum?"

Nancy stiffened, terminating her chewing. A few students began to snicker.

"Nancy," Mr. Thomas said, "You can eliminate that bubble and swallow that gum."

Nancy rose from her seat and swallowed her gum before the entire class. She, then, sat back down.

Certainly, the math class was off to an entertaining start, but soon resumed into its normal, tedious state with the teacher resuming his lecture and demonstrations until the bell sounded again, ending the class. Paul collected his books and Nancy's, and the couple went to their next class together. Not surprisingly, math class was not considered to be a challenging class for Paul, unlike his peers. His family often worked with different types of math at his family's business called Sal's Country Store: a business that had been passed down for generations. It was now owned by his grandfather, Abraham Boudreaux, who was Paul's legal guardian after both his parents passed away in a car accident while he was young and barely in middle school. Sadly, his grandfather was now hospitalized with his health slowly deteriorating. Paul had a great relationship with his grandfather, but that connection made his other family members loathe Paul. It was no secret that the old man wanted to leave everything to him. Knowing that it was forming animosity between the rest of the family, Paul beseeched his grandfather to divide everything evenly between everyone, but the old man refused, affirming that none of them deserved it as much as he. Yet, not wanting to make things worse for himself, Paul made secret agreements to other members of the family that once Abraham passed, he would see to it that they would all still get a fair share of the assets. So far, it seemed to work, but their abhorrence still fermented from within.

"You still want to go to the drive-in on Friday?" Paul asked Nancy, draping his free arm around her shoulder.

"Sure," Nancy replied, intertwining her fingers in his as they went into their next class.

Paul passed Nancy her books and sat down next to her, as he did in all their classes together. Henry, who sat behind him, tapped Paul's shoulder with his hand. Paul turned around and saw Henry pull out a hidden car magazine. The magazine was folded to a page that had a blue vehicle, leather interior, and white wall tires. Paul's eyes widened at the luxurious looking vehicle that had the whopping price of $2500! Paul's eyes quickly scanned the magazine to see how fast that sharp, beauty would drive, but the bell rang again, and Henry quickly hid the magazine between the rest of his books.

Paul turned around and reclined in his chair. The next teacher introduced the same Negro girl again. It was getting annoying because Paul already had the same girl in his previous class and the teachers were announcing her like she was some big shot celebrity. Nell stood with no confidence and appeared to be a square. *She cannot even look people in the face, no wonder she doesn't know anything and can't make friends. How could you learn anything by staring at the floor all day?* Paul examined the girl's face closer, leaning slightly forward. *Hmmm...She has an attractive face and beautiful lips.* Paul speculated what they felt like: *like soft pillows*, but immediately pushed those unnatural thoughts from his mind. Nell was colored and it wasn't normal for a white guy to think such thoughts. *There is a reason why God made separate races and hers is inferior.*

The teacher requested Paul to distribute papers and as Paul was doing so, he ultimately stood by Nell. She seemed so virtuous and fearful, making Paul feel more powerful. He already had such clout over all the other students, but Nell appeared even more vulnerable than they did. Paul found that reality to be somewhat humorous. He chuckled to himself at the notion of how the media perceived the Negro people like her as threats to whites. Paul never had many encounters with Negro people himself, but if they were anything like Nell, there certainly was nothing to worry about. As far as he was concerned, she was beneath him.

During lunchtime, Paul and his friends were assembled in the cafeteria, eating their food. Today's meal consisted of spaghetti, green salad, fruit, and milk. The girls carefully ate their food, while the guys dug into their food with less care, especially Bill, who had already spilled a few chunks of sauce onto himself. He did not fit in with the group at all and it was well known that the only reason why the others were tolerating him, and his presence was because he was Paul's cousin and someone who would follow Nancy around, like a rejected puppy. To everyone within the group, Bill was viewed as nothing short of a gnat. Therefore, most of the group did what they did best: ignore him and continued their talks of the day. The entire school was talking about the Negro students. Each grade ranging from the 10th grade to the 12th grade had new Negro students. The 10th graders had the most with at least five and the 12th grade class had the least with two students. Even though there had been no misgivings, there was still this belief that the new students needed to go somewhere else and were not welcomed.

"They just don't belong here," Henry said, irritation in his voice. "Yeah, their school burned down, but the colored students could just use another building in their own community or go to another colored school in another town. Everywhere they go, there is always trouble. Why can't they just stay in their spaces and leave ours alone?"

"I don't feel safe with any of them here with us," another student chimed in.

"Maybe if we give them a hard enough time, they will go away," a girl whispered. "I heard that worked the last time the school had to take them. If it worked before, it should work again."

"I just want things to go back to being normal," Nancy said. "I say that we should at least keep our school events strictly for us. They can always have their own events, separately. What do you think, Pau?"

"That should help get rid of them for the most part, but we are still screwed for classes," Paul said. "English, history, and science are classes that are big on group projects, which means we have to work with them."

"Great," a boy groaned, "our grades will probably tank because of them."

"Maybe some of them are smart," another boy declared.

The group laughed.

"*None* of them are smart," Bill replied. "If they were smart, they never would have come here in the first place."

"Let's just agree that when it comes to schoolwork and projects, to just go with it," Paul suggested. "We don't want the teachers to get on our cases about them. It will just mean that we will probably have to end up doing most of the projects ourselves without their help. Afterall, we want to maintain our grades, so we don't fail our senior year."

The group nodded in agreement and finished their meal. On his way out of the cafeteria, Bill let out a colossal belch, grossing out several people in the cafeteria. Paul exhaled, contemplating why he was related to such a vile creature such as Bill. If Bill weren't so strong, Paul would have expelled him from the group a long time ago, but everyone was afraid of Bill, including Paul who was increasingly losing patience with him. When Paul would discuss his detest about Bill to their grandfather, Abraham, the old man would tell Paul to have more patience with Bill because he was strong, and that strength would become useful for his protection one day. Irritated, Paul exited the cafeteria.

"Hey, Paul," Henry whispered in the hallway.

Paul turned his way and Henry beckoned him towards the lockers away from their group of friends. Both teens went to Henry's locker and he unlocked it. Henry pulled out a rubber snake and shoved it into his pocket. He pressed a finger to his lips and the teens sprinted down the hallway.

"I knew this would come in handy one day," Henry said. "Which locker is that colored girl's?"

"I don't know, it could be any of these," Paul replied.

"Darn," Henry said. "Don't you have another class with her?"

"At the rate that it's going, I might."

"Good, take it and scare her with it," Henry took the rubber snake out of his pocket and passed it to Paul, who shoved it into his. Both boys went their separate ways, going to their next class. Fortunately, Paul's next class included Nell and he enthusiastically volunteered to pass out the assignment. Not suspecting anything, the teacher granted Paul permission to distribute the papers. Barely able to suppress his laughter, Paul gleefully began to deliver the papers to each student. Finally reaching Nell's desk, Paul cautiously pulled out the rubber snake and dropped it onto Nell's desk, promptly moving as if nothing happened. With her eyes no longer on the floor and now on her desk, noticing the snake, Nell shrieked. She leapt from her desk, knocking it over as several students gasped and pushed away from her, pondering what all the commotion was about. Paul burst into laughter once the teacher hurried towards Nell and books began to fly and hit the floor with futile attempts to kill the rubber snake. Several girls screamed and shoved their fellow classmates out of their way, in an unpleasant attempt to get away from the horrible creature. Several boys threw their books and stomped on the snake until the vibrations from their stomps sent it flying into the air, making the anxieties of other classmates worse. One girl shoved a boy forward, making him fall to the floor near the snake. The boy cried out as his arm hit the floor. Finally, one of the students grumbled and grabbed the fake snake.

"It's not even real," the student shouted, holding the snake in the air for the rest of the class to see.

Realizing it was a prank, a few students began to laugh, while others appeared annoyed and went back to their seats. Enraged, the teacher demanded to know who placed the rubber snake on Nell's desk. With no response, the teacher stated that should another prank take place and the perpetrator caught, he or she would be in big trouble. Paul snickered at the feeble threat. He gawked to the back of the classroom and saw that Nell's eyes were no longer fixed on the floor. She was glaring to the front of the class, angry and humiliated. His mission was accomplished.

During after school dismissal, Paul was more than ecstatic to notify Henry of the events that transpired during class. In fact, both Paul and Henry were laughing so much that both youths were crying tears. In the mist of his laughter, Paul spotted Nell angrily marching to her car in the parking lot. It was an old and rusty car that looked like it would break down at any minute. She flung open the door, hurled her books into the back seat, and slammed the door shut. It was all a fun game to Paul. School had been boring, minus the sporting and dance events. Now, he had something more to look forward to, at the expense of Nell and several of the other Negro students.

Chapter 2

Henry placed the cigarette between his lips and took one last puff. That was the end of it. He smashed it in the ashtray. Paul waved the smoke away from himself and out the window. The rest of the teens in the backseat of Henry's family's old junky car were flipping through magazines that either had pictures of cars or women. In five minutes, the school bell would ring, starting a new day. Most students hung around outside of the school on the benches, the lawn, their vehicles, or the sidewalk.

"You're going to screw around and have us all smelling like smoke," Paul told his friend.

"Most of the teachers smoke," Henry retorted. "We can just put the blame back on them or another adult." He grabbed an adult magazine from his stack of magazines and began smirking at the pictures of the ladies.

"You guys going to the race this weekend?" one of the jocks in the backseat asked.

"Nah," said Henry, "I'm gonna be back here helpin' Mr. Payne work on more vehicles."

Mr. Payne was the auto mechanic teacher who taught at Wood Oak High School. Every Saturday from 8 a.m. to 1 p.m., he and several students would work on cars and trucks on campus. Sometimes the students would work on their own vehicles or their parents' vehicles. It was not a requirement to be there, but lots of students enjoyed working on cars and the auto mechanic class had been the most popular class for the male students for years.

"How much is the prize money at the race this week?" Paul asked.

"Five hundred for first place, three hundred for second, and two hundred for third," the other jock said. "I would go, but my older brother has the car this weekend and my dad wants me to help him do some dumb yard work."

Henry whistled at the news about the prize money. He came from a poor family and any chance to make a quick, easy buck often got his attention. However, most teens used their regular cars or an old car to race at the stock car racetrack, but his vehicle wouldn't be ready in time for the weekend, so he had to opt out.

"What's your weekend lookin' like, Paul?" Henry inquired.

"I'm gonna visit my grandfather first and then go work at the store," Paul said. "You know how strict he is. We all have to pull our weight." Paul put the car magazine down and peered out the window, scanning the parking lot. Not too far from Henry's car was Nell's car.

Paul's eyes lit up with excitement, as the adrenaline rushed through him. He watched Nell and a younger Negro girl exit the vehicle. His smirk gradually receded when he saw the younger Negro girl run towards a young white girl. Expecting a fight, Paul began to prepare himself to defend the white girl. If the Negro students wanted a race war, he would be more than happy to give them one. After all, they were nothing but trouble and his family knew how to deal with the likes of them. Fuming, Paul balled his fist and prepared to leave Henry's car until he saw something unexpected. Briefly, both girls embraced each other! Then, laughing, they entered the building talking to one another as Nell followed. Paul was dumbstruck. *Why would they be doing something like that?* The girls, at least the younger two, were friends. *A white girl and a Negro girl!*

The school bell sounded, and Paul and his friends got out of Henry's car. More curious than ever, Paul crept away from his cluster of friends. He observed all three girls continue their walk towards the lockers of the 10th grade students. There were more Negro students in that area, a tiny group of five, and they talked to the white girl as if she were no different from them. Unmistakably, there was some sort of friendship, and it was something Paul never imagined seeing for himself at Wood Oak High School.

Nell talked briefly to the small group of 10th graders, before departing. Paul pressed his back against the lockers, hiding within the crowd of students, wondering if what he had believed and done to her earlier had been the right or wrong thing. After all he had put her through, Nell did not take any vengeful actions towards people like him as he had anticipated.

Maybe she is just weak, Paul thought, now sitting in his homeroom class. Or maybe she and the other Negro *students plan on using that white girl or are just waiting for her to let her guard down to later attack her...*He snuck a glance to the back of the classroom. Nell certainly didn't look like she was planning anything malice. Like the rest of the class, she was busy arranging her books and papers for the day while the homeroom teacher was taking attendance. Sitting next to her,

Martin was doing the same. Paul turned back around and started preparing his own materials for the day. A few of the other students were talking about the afterschool prep rally, but Paul still had his mind preoccupied on what he had seen and the mindset that he was raised to believe. When homeroom ended, he took his time getting to his next class, continuing to ponder.

Still guilt stricken, Paul sulked as he entered into the math classroom. He spotted Nell sitting in her desk with her eyes once again glued to the floor, annoying him. Now, he despised what he was witnessing and wanted to tell her to stop looking so pathetic but remained hushed as several students pushed past him to get to their seats. Paul got into his and the teacher revealed that there would be a pop quiz, much to the shock of many of the students. Surprisingly, the teacher requested for Paul to deliver the papers once again. As he was doing so, Paul inadvertently locked eyes with Nell. Startled that she was no longer staring at the floor and directly at *him*, Paul took a slight step back before giving her a paper. His heart almost leapt out of his chest and his face became flushed with redness. He quickly returned to his seat. Sitting back down, Paul took a deep breath and exhaled. Nell's glance scared *him*, and *she* was considered the weakest person in the entire class. She managed to make him feel smaller than *her* for a moment. Paul couldn't comprehend how someone like him could have ever permitted that to happen but was relieved that none of his peers had seen the moment. Maybe because Nell did something unexpected or maybe because she figured out that he was the one who pulled the prank on her. Either way, she took some of his power and cockiness away from him. Incensed, Paul gazed outside the window to calm his nerves. It was getting bleaker and cloudy outside.

After school, it was time to go back to the family store. It had been productive and less tedious with the radio playing in the background. Paul began to whistle and snap his fingers to the music playing on the radio. After the crazy day he had at school, even he was thankful to be working that evening. Music and dancing had always had a profound, loving place in his heart. It reminded him of the memorable times he had with his mother. At times, when Paul closed his eyes, he could see her smiling down at him, as before, once upon a time. He remembered the captivating floral scent of her perfume as she took his hand, teaching him the dances she often did with his father.

"One day, you're going to make a lucky woman very happy," his mother said, beaming at her son, who was seven years old at the time.

Paul smiled as he lifted his arm high, still shorter than her. Giggling, Paul's mother lowered herself, almost slightly kneeling as she tried to spin underneath. Rising back to her height, they continued the dance until the song ended. Merrily, his mother kissed his cheek.

"Will she be like you?" Paul asked.

"Better than me," his mother stated.

"How will I know?"

"You will know. If you love her just as much as your father and I love each other."

It was getting late and storming outside, but Paul and his cousin, Bill, managed to stay later than usual at the family store. Bill announced that he was leaving and left Paul to close the shop alone. Paul exhaled with relief and a little bit of exhaustion. By completing their duties, he and Bill wouldn't have to fret about working Friday to stock shelves or take inventory. Anytime the cousins knew they wanted to pursue other interests; they were required to spend extra time at the store the day before. It had always been planned that way, as ordered by their grandfather. With everything in its place, Paul turned off the radio and turned off the lights. Stepping outside and locking the door, Paul grimaced as the rain fell heavily over his jacket and himself. He scurried to get into his well-kept red and white vehicle that had been given to him a year ago as a birthday present from his grandfather. Suddenly, another vehicle pulled over next to his. Paul could barely make out the old, rusty vehicle between the bolts of lightning and heavy rain.

"Wait," the person called out, "Please, I need help!"

"The store is closed," Paul answered. "Come back tomorrow!"

He climbed into his vehicle and shut the door. Then, he heard rapid knocks to his car window, infuriating him. Paul wanted to go home and fast. He was weary and the weather was terrible outside.

"Please," the person begged, "I need help."

Paul considered driving away and disregarding the stranger but thought about the situation. Yes, he was fatigued, but someone was in need during a storm and a terrible one at that. He was still able to go home, but the other person would be trapped at the mercy of the weather and from the looks of it, the weather was in an even more cranky mood than he was. Feeling a little more compassionate, Paul opened the car door and pushed past the person. Paul pulled his jacket slightly over his head and made his way back to the entrance of the store. Unlocking the door, he and the person entered. Paul flicked on the lights, revealing that he was once again with his classmate, Nell Jefferson. Both stood together, drenched in rainwater. Paul contemplated why Nell would decide to stop by his family's business of all places, but as tired as he was, he wanted to get things over with so he could go home and sleep.

"What's the problem?" Paul asked, wiping some of the rainwater from his face.

"My car got a flat tire," Nell said. "I had no choice but to stop here...Aren't you, Paul Boudreaux?"

"Yeah, I'm Paul Boudreaux. This is my grandfather's store. I look familiar because we go to the same school...Let me go out and look at your car."

"Thanks, I really appreciate it."

Paul grabbed several tools from behind the counter. Leaving the store, he began working on the vehicle and pulled off the flat. He had forgotten to ask Nell if she had a spare tire, and it didn't seem like she had one from the looks of it. Luckily, his family's store had spare tires that could probably serve as a good replacement. Unfortunately, on how strict his grandfather was about store merchandise, the tire would still need to be paid for. Paul doubted that Nell would probably have the extra funds to pay the cost of the tire on such short notice. He deliberated on how the tire would be reimbursed, when he thought of paying for it himself. After all, he still felt somewhat remorseful of bullying Nell and maybe him replacing the tire could serve as a way for him to clear his conscience. Paul examined her old tire and went out to the back of the store and got a similar one and replaced it. Still soaking wet, he entered the store once again. He grabbed a towel from behind the counter and got rid of the mud and water that covered his face and hands. He put the tools away and began to sneeze. He grabbed the tab notebook and made a note to deduct the cost of the tire from his earnings.

"I'm sorry," said Nell. "You are probably going to catch a cold for helping me. I'm really sorry. How much do I owe you?"

"It's no big deal," Paul said. "Your tire has been replaced. Don't worry about it. I just got to get home. I'll see you out."

He waited for her to get into her car before returning into his. He sneezed once again before driving back home.

Chapter 3

Tonight, was going to be the first football game of the season and all of the students were enthused. Excitedly, Paul and Henry began tossing a football back and forth, taking shots at each other, and teasing one another about past fails and successes. Nancy was busy talking to the cheerleaders that morning, so she and Paul didn't do of their usual make out sessions that morning, making Paul a little disheartened. He sneezed once again and excused himself from the group. His nose was beginning to run, and he needed to get some tissue. He went into the boy's restroom, gathered some tissue, blew his nose, and shoved some extra tissue into his pocket. He prayed that his cold wouldn't screw things up for the game. The last thing he wanted was for Henry and the other guys to give him some lip over fumbling the ball because he sneezed. He would never hear the end of it! Striding down the hallway, Paul stopped as Nell approached him, appearing tense naturally. Almost trembling, she raised a small, covered plate towards him.

"What's *that*?" Paul asked suspiciously.

"I brought you some pound cake," Nell said. "To thank you for helping me the other day." She gradually lifted her eyes from the floor, showing deep brown eyes that had a unique sweetness about them. Paul was taken aback. Those eyes were exceedingly beautiful. Paul's eyes trailed down to Nell's luscious full lips and strangely, Paul could see himself becoming entranced with desiring to press his lips against hers. Mesmerized, Paul smiled slightly at her gentle eyes and the thoughtful gesture.

"You brought *me* pound cake?" he asked, amazed, his heart filling with elation.

"Yes."

Abruptly, Paul realized Bill was moving down the hallway. Befuddled, Bill stared at Paul and Nell. Panicked, Paul turned again to Nell, swiftly eradicating his smile and any sentimental thoughts.

"I don't want it," Paul stated, turning around and moving away. He was astonished by the gesture from Nell. It was pleasant, but he couldn't be seen socializing with a square like her. Plus, not to mention that she was a Negro. If his family and friends ever found out that he was on friendly terms with someone like her, there could be no telling what would happen. It could ruin his reputation throughout the entire school and most likely, the community. She was attractive in his eyes, but he couldn't risk himself for the likes of someone like her. She already had a target on her back by everyone in his group of friends. Knowing them, even if he were to say something, they would probably think of him in another light, branding him a deserter to his own race.

Paul walked into the math class and sat down to take the test that Mr. Thomas has scheduled for the day. The new formula was incredibly long and difficult to remember. A few students stared blankly at their test papers as if they had already given up. Luckily for Paul, he had memorized the formula by writing it down several times before school started. Nancy flipped her paper to the next page and began working on easier formulas. Bill began to write down random numbers on his test. Lastly, Henry began mouthing to himself to recollect the formulas from his memory. The classroom was completely mute, and confusion filled the air. Minutes went by as the clock ticked away shortening the time of the test. Mr. Thomas quietly stepped between Paul and the student seated across from him on the right.

"David," Mr. Thomas whispered to the student, "Let me see your hand."

The rest of the class turned to face both the teacher and the student. The student named David Hebert reluctantly raised his hand to the teacher. Slowly, Mr. Thomas began reading the math formula out loud from the student's hand. Henry and a few students gasped and quickly began to jot down the formula. David grimaced and Mr. Thomas took his test back to the front of the classroom. He pulled out a red pen from his desk and everyone knew what would happen next: David was going to receive a zero on the test and get a detention. Unfortunately for him, it was his first time receiving a detention, which meant that his parents would be notified, and he would have to spend thirty minutes with Mr. Thomas after school that day. David partially covered his face with his hands and the rest of the class resumed taking their test.

Paul nervously bit down on his pencil when suddenly, there was a light bump against Paul's shoe, breaking him from his concentration. A pencil laid on the floor next to him. Paul peeked to the back of the classroom. All the other students were hard at work on their papers, except Nell who was looking at him with a plea in her eyes. *It was her pencil!* Paul didn't want to be in the same awkward position again. He couldn't just helpfully hand Nell the pencil back without looking like he was friends with her. Instead, he took the liberty to kick the pencil further away from himself and refocused back onto his own paper. Paul knew that what he was doing was heartless and unjustified towards her, but he owed her nothing, not even his respect.

During lunch, Paul beamed with satisfaction at his tray of meatloaf, mashed potatoes and gravy, and mixed vegetables. Meatloaf was one of his favorite foods and it couldn't have come at a better time. He was getting anxious about the game and wanting to impress the scouts. He wondered if some of the big shot universities would pick him to join their teams; then, he could make a name for himself on campus with the possibilities of going pro upon graduation.

"I know this sounds bad but I'm glad David was caught cheating," Henry confessed. "I couldn't remember that first formula to save my life and it was half of the test! Mr. Thomas must be sadistic!"

"How do you know if what he wrote was even accurate?" another jock asked. "You know David's handwriting is barely legible. Even he can barely read it!"

"Mr. Thomas read it out loud to the class, so it must have been correct," Nancy stated.

"It sounded correct to me," said Paul. "But you do know that math isn't going to be getting any easier, so you might as well start remembering those formulas. If your grades go down, the coaches will make you sit out for the game and this is the worst time to be benched with the scouts starting to show up. Remember when Freddy Kleinpeter sat out years ago and messed up his whole team?"

"That was the first time Wood Oak had a losing streak for the football games," Henry reflected. "That team was the worst. All we ever heard was how much the team fumbled the ball. Their only good player was Freddy! The rest couldn't run or catch!"

"But *we* can," Paul said enthusiastically. "We are going to go to district, regional, and state!"

The table of friends cheered vociferously and picked up their empty trays to return to the cafeteria staff. The rest of the students in the cafeteria grinned at the excited group as the team began to goof off during their departure. The group soon came upon the table where the Negro students were sitting. Paul and his friends surrounded the duo and began to cough over their food. Roaring with laughter, the popular students stormed out the cafeteria.

Later that night, it was time to handle business. Paul and the rest of the football team wanted their first game to be successful. As expected, Paul, the quarterback, received the ball from the center. Fading back, he passed the ball, which was caught by the end, scoring a touchdown. After several plays, the crowd cheered wildly because of the Wood Oak High School team winning of 28 to 7. It was believed that this win predicted an excellent season.

After the winning game, Paul and Nancy drove to the local drive-in movie theater, The Movie Pit. It was a popular drive-in where most of the community would hang out after the high school games. Friday nights were frequented by hungry, horny teens and their dates. It was uncommon for any of the couples to participate in *watching* the movies, making the theater obtain the label as "The Tongue Pit." Often an untamed place during Friday nights, the theater had to employ a substantial number of staff to help sustain the grounds, food stand, and guests. Several teens had abandoned their vehicles and were socializing near the concession stand or on the hoods of their friends' cars. Taking advantage of another opportunity to make out, Paul draped his arm around Nancy and the pair began to do their usual make out session. Paul enjoyed kissing girls and Nancy was the type of girl that would allow him to do whatever he wanted with her. In fact, they had already gone all the way and even then, Paul still gave her everything but his heart and his school ring to officially seal the deal that the two would finally be going steady. Paul considered giving Nancy his ring, but deep down, he knew that he didn't love her. Love was something that his parents had, and he didn't see that with Nancy. He knew that Nancy loved him, but he never told her that he loved her, and he still wasn't sure if he did. It would have been easy for him to tell her those three words without meaning them, but Paul could never bring himself to tell *any* girl such words. *Why buy the cow when you can get the milk for free?*

Ending the kiss, Paul peered at the screen to watch what was left of the movie. His stomach began to growl. *A tasty hotdog and a soda could fix that.* Paul was just about to order some food when he saw *her. Since when did Nell work at the drive-in?* She was in her work uniform, as she traveled back and forth between the concession stand and the cars. Paul gawked at her sensual, almost pouty lips once again, fantasizing about what they would feel like. Again, he pushed those thoughts out of his mind and left the car to order his food. The concession stand had a long line and was swamped. The teens behind the counter had run out of fresh popcorn and hot dogs. A frustrated teen worker sighed as she hurried to make more popcorn and hotdogs. The manager who was known as "Douglas" began writing orders as another teen worker angrily began counting money to give a customer her change from the register. When Douglas got to Paul, Paul gave him his order and information on where to find him during the chaos. Paul paid for his order and returned to his vehicle.

"What happened, Paul?" Nancy asked.

"They are making more food and it's going to be a while," Paul informed her, closing the door to the car. Returning to their make out session, Paul forgot about his order until he heard someone clearing her throat near his window. Paul broke his kiss with Nancy and saw Nell standing by his window with the food that he had ordered. Paul grabbed the tray, gave Nancy a bucket of popcorn and put the other food and drink items on the dashboard. For a moment, Paul caught a whiff of an alluring scent. It smelled of a light, peaceful, floral aroma and it was coming from Nell. *Why does she smell so good?* Snapping back to reality and angry at himself for being charmed by her, Paul took the tray and shoved it out the window. The tray fell to the ground between Nell and Paul's vehicle. With composure, Nell lowered herself to the ground to retrieve the tray and stormed off.

"That wasn't very nice, Paul," Nancy stated, taking a sip of her drink.

"Don't worry about her," Paul said. "Worry about what's going to happen with us once we leave here." He wrapped his arm around Nancy's shoulder again. Unexpectedly,

Paul spotted Nell returning to the front of his car with a large cup in her hand. Her once bashful eyes were now filled with rage and disgust. She approached Paul's window with the cup and hurled its contents on him. Astounded by the coldness of the soda and the act itself, Paul cried out.

"What the heck?" Paul exclaimed, alerting Nancy. "Hey!"

"What are you doing?" Nancy demanded, eyeballing Nell and her drenched boyfriend.

"Have a nice day," Nell stated, flashing a mocking smirk, and taking off.

Paul was now infuriated. Nell had humiliated him in front of his date and possibly ruined the interior of his car. He squinted his eyes, zoning in on her as the adrenaline rushed through his veins. Paul unlocked the door and stormed after her. Onlookers began to laugh and point at him as he raged after her in his soda-soaked pants. Catching up to her, Paul snatched the back of Nell's arm, forgetting himself momentarily. He glowered at her as the words escaped his mouth.

"You're going to pay for that," Paul said, tightening his grip.

"Get your hands off of me," Nell shouted, grimacing.

"Paul," Nancy called out, approaching them, "what is going on? Why did she dump soda on you?"

"Because he is rude," Nell said.

"The one who is rude is *you*," Nancy fired back. "You should be fired from your job. You don't treat customers like this. I would like to speak to your manager."

"Fine," Nell said jerking her arm away from Paul's grip. They all entered the building where Nell was reprimanded by the manager. Paul and Nancy went back to his car and began cleaning the mess from the spill. In a fit of fury, Paul cussed loudly about how his car was now ruined. He balled up several soaked pieces of paper towels and hurled it to the ground. Several football players and cheerleaders from Wood Oak High School approached the car. Other teens sat quietly, watching from the hoods of their cars.

"What happened?" one of the cheerleaders asked.

"That girl dumped soda all over Paul and ruined our date," Nancy said, her eyes brimming with tears. She sniffed back a small sob and one of her friends embraced her, trying to provide comfort.

"I told you people like them ruin everything," another girl reminded them.

"We can get her at school on Monday," one of the other jocks exclaimed.

"Just drop it already!" Paul yelled. "We're leaving! Get inside the car, Nancy!"

He slammed the car door shut and gripped the steering wheel tightly. Still weeping, Nancy reentered the vehicle and closed the door. Losing his temper by the second, Paul pressed his foot to the pedal, almost swerving erratically out of the movie parking lot. They drove near the employee parking lot and Paul spotted Nell getting into her own car. Paul veered his car into the lot, preventing Nell's car from departing. Paul heatedly blew his horn, eager to intimidate her.

"Paul, let's just go," Nancy called out, but Paul had already exited the vehicle. He slammed his door shut and marched to the driver's side of Nell's car. He struck the window with his fists. Terrified, Nell let out a bloodcurdling cry and scooted away from the door.

"You want to dump soda on me?" Paul demanded, kicking the side of Nell's vehicle. "You want to fight? Come on!"

"Paul, stop," Nancy said rushing out of Paul's vehicle and clutching his arm. "It was just soda! Let's go, okay?"

"Not until she gets what's coming to her," Paul bellowed giving Nell's car another swift kick.

"Help!" Nell shouted, pressing her car horn, bursting into tears.

The parking lot began to fill with patrons as both Nancy and Nell began to cry hysterically. Finally, Paul yanked his arm from Nancy's grip and got back into his vehicle. A bawling Nancy pursued Paul back into the car before it sped away down the street.

Chapter 4

The following Monday, word traveled quickly about the quarrel at the drive-in with most of the cheerleaders and jocks scheming vengeance against Nell. Throughout the day, she had been shoved, cursed at, and bullied. Unfortunately, Bill heard about the situation, and he was furious. Paul was still bitter, but his fury had diminished greatly during the weekend. Luckily, he managed to remove the soda stains from his vehicle before they set. He refused to talk to anyone about the situation at school, but other students continued to talk and plot. Bill vowed to get back at Nell at the end of the school day, putting Paul on high alert. Knowing how overprotective Bill was about Nancy, Paul did everything possible to try to calm his cousin down before they both could figure out where Nell had gone after school. Her car was still in the parking lot, but it was empty. Paul trailed Bill throughout the school, room after room. Paul had football practice that day, but he continued to follow his cousin.

"I'm gonna beat her with my bare hands," Bill yelled as he burst into several classrooms, searching for his target. The cousins searched the school, all while an infuriated Bill was beginning to punch the lockers with his fists, denting them. Paul knew that the longer Bill was upset, the worst he became. If Paul didn't calm Bill down, he was more than capable of carrying out his promises.

"She didn't even do anything to Nancy," Paul said, following Bill.

"She made Nancy cry; that's enough for me," Bill hollered, shoving a bystander out of his way.

"Just let me handle it," Paul suggested. "You are down to your last suspension. If you get one more, you'll get expelled, then you won't be able to see Nancy at school anymore!"

Bill stopped in his tracks; his fists were still balled. If there was one thing that was Bill's greatest fear, it was losing Nancy. It was enough that Bill had failed to win her affections, but the idea of him getting kicked out of school and never being around her as often as he liked was a situation that even he couldn't take.

"I'm still gonna make sure she never messes with Nancy ever again," Bill uttered, entering the library.

Paul momentarily held his breath once they spotted Nell. She was sitting deep within the back of the library. She had her focus transfixed in a book with a pencil in hand to take notes. Luckily, Paul had convinced Bill to calm down before things could have gotten worse. Bill grabbed Nell's pencil and threw it across the aisle. Petrified at the sight of the two cousins, Nell froze.

"So, I heard what happened Friday night," Bill said, leaning against the table. It moved slightly from his weight.

Nell appeared terrified, even beginning to tremble. By now, all the Negro students had heard the rumors about how dangerous Bill could be. Most students, including whites, did not dare to get on his bad side. The last student that was rumored to have gotten into a fight with Bill had to be admitted into a hospital and was still out of school recovering. He had broken the student's ribs and nose because the teen was foolish enough to call Bill a skuzz. Bill began to crack the knuckles of his enlarged hands.

"You think you can just go around disrespecting white folks," he said. "Well, I got news for you, you colored bitch. You mess with one of us, you have a problem with *all* of us. If I ever see you around that drive-in again, it'll be the last time that anyone ever sees you."

Nell persisted to stare at the table, and Bill glowered at her with a deadly, icy glimpse. He stood there for a while, daringly waiting for her to confront him. Seeing that she was not going to challenge him, he momentarily stepped away, but not before calling her every rude name in the book. He slammed the library door shut behind him.

Paul lingered behind, observing that Nell was on the brink of tears. As horrendous as the encounter was with Bill, Paul figured that Nell had gotten off easily compared to everyone he had seen in the past. They were alone in the library, except for the librarian who often stayed in the front. Still sour, Paul folded his arms across his chest and leaned against her table. He listened as she sniffled. *Cry all you want; it could have been worse.*

"What are you going to do now?" Paul asked, acrimoniously. "You don't have any soda today."

Nell said nothing and dropped her eyes in the same submissive stance as the first day of class.

"So, you're scared now," Paul acknowledged.

Nell raised her eyes once more, a glimpse of defeat in them. Paul expected that from her. She was the weakling that he knew she was. *What an uptight flake! Maybe she didn't have any fire within her after all. She was just some boring girl who let people walk all over her. If that were the case, maybe she deserved to be treated poorly.* Suddenly, Nell's lips curled as she spat in his face, stunning Paul. Appalled, Paul took a step back as he wiped the spit from his eyes. He glared at her as he wiped the spit onto the book that she was reading. He wasn't sure if he wanted to fight her or if he gained a new sense of respect towards her.

"For someone who is colored, you got a lot of nerve spitting in a white person's face," Paul said. "You weren't brave enough to do it to Bill. Looks like I don't scare you enough." He wiped his hand on his pants.

"Get away from me, you white devil," Nell said, trying to suppress her anger.

"White devil?" Paul said, mockingly. "Yet, you offered me, a white devil, pound cake not too long ago."

"Yeah, when you weren't an ass," Nell said.

"If I'm a devil, I should be an ass," Paul said. "I don't want to disappoint your expectations of me." He leaned forward slightly as Nell leaned back, testing her once again. He knew she was still scared of him, but this time, her eyes had that fiery resentment that he was relishing.

"You're the one who kicked my pencil and threw the tray to the ground," Nell reminded him. "You were rude first. What do you expect? I'm not going to respect or be nice to people who are like you, especially since you are being rude because I'm black."

Paul paused and gazed at the clock on the library wall. It was almost time for the library to close.

"You aren't as innocent as you think you are," he told her. "You ruined my date, dumped soda on me, spit in my face, and called me a white devil. You're just as prejudiced and no better than I am."

Nell groaned and slammed her book shut. She rose to her feet and pushed past Paul. She rushed out of the library, followed by him. Paul chuckled as he ran past her to the driver's door of her car. Nell stopped and moved towards the opposite side, but Paul got there first. Nell tried to go to the other side, but he beat her once again. He laughed out loud, thrilled.

"Don't you have anything else better to do?" Nell demanded.

"No," Paul said.

Nell eyed the parking lot, realizing they were alone and reminding her that she was helpless. She slowly backed away from the car as Paul began to move towards her with each step.

"I did a good job fixing your tire," he stated. "I want to be rewarded properly."

"What do you mean by *that*?" Nell asked, more frightened than ever.

"Not out here," Paul said. He nodded back towards her car, taking steps back towards it until he was inches away from the driver's side. *You want to ruin my car and my date; I'm going to scare you so bad that you will pee on yourself in your own car. Then I can make you look like an idiot, just like you did to me!*

Nell was scared and saw more students walking into the parking lot to their cars. Feeling a little more at ease and wanting to take the opportunity, she swiftly took out her keys and unlocked her door. As she climbed in, Paul sauntered to the passenger side. He knocked on the door as Nell started the car.

"Remember that I helped you," he reminded her.

Paul watched as Nell burst into tears, clutching the steering wheel. Her chest quivered and her body shook as she reluctantly opened the car door. Paul climbed inside and shut the door. Now holding herself, Nell avoided looking at him as her chest continued to tremble between sobs. Her face was wet, and the tears fell from her face, soaking her shirt. Immediately, Paul began to feel guilty about everything that he had done, now realizing how much it had affected her. He knew that he and his friends had greatly wronged her by calling her slurs, shoving her, and treating her like someone who was less than human. Things had gotten out of hand and he wanted to tell her that he was sorry, but even, then, he thought she may never want to listen to what he had to say. Not knowing what else to do, he reached down and attempted to touch her hand, but Nell let out a small shriek that disturbed him deep to his core. Paul struggled to fight back his own tears, feeling horrible for all that he had done. He couldn't even look her in the eyes anymore and listened to the moral death sentence that he had placed upon himself towards his own prejudiced ways as he listened to her sobs. Momentarily, the parking lot emptied, and they were alone again. Nell's hysteria eventually subsided and Paul, now disgusted with himself and remorseful, turned her way. He pulled his hand away, opened the door and stepped out. He closed the door and went to his car and sat inside.

"What kind of person am *I*?" Paul asked himself, clutching the wheel of his car. "I can't believe what I've done. I'm such a jerk. I don't know if I can ever forgive myself for what I've done to her."

Chapter 5

The next day fared no better for Nell, who was still being mistreated by the popular teens, apart from Paul. Still recollecting her cries, he refused to continue to participate in any activity that involved mistreating Nell or the other Negro students. Martin, the other 12th grade Negro student, began to hide out in different parts of the school to avoid conflict with the other seniors. Whenever some of the jocks managed to find him hiding in bathroom stalls or other parts of the school building, they would shove him into the lockers and lock him inside, hurl papers at him, and call him as many insensitive racial slurs as they could think of. The cheerleaders were just as brutal to Nell; they would intentionally step on her shoes, shove her, grab at her hair, and call her racial slurs. Negro students were the targets of these harsh behaviors done by white students from all three grade levels (sophomores, juniors, and seniors). Most teachers were able to stop the brawls in many of the classrooms.

Repentant of his past aggressions, Paul wanted to at least inform Nell how regretful he was for all that he had put her through. He knew that she had begun to be more cautious around the other students, especially white ones. Hurt, Nell seldom participated in class and even during group assignments, she never spoke much. Paul waited until the end of the school day, hoping to find her at the library. He was aware that he would get in trouble for missing practice again. He still had time, Coach Anderson didn't mind if players were a few minutes late, but he had completely missed practice yesterday and knew that the coach would be questioning him when he returned to the field. Today, Paul was determined to go to practice, but morally, he needed to talk to Nell and apologize for yesterday and the bullying from days prior, no matter the costs. Inside the library, Paul sat down with Nancy next to him. Anxiously, Nancy tapped her feet on the floor.

"I can't miss practice," Nancy said.

"I understand," Paull said. He gave her a quick smooch.

The door to the library opened and Nell walked past them to the back of the library. Nancy rose to her feet and went out of the library. Paul followed Nell to a table. He pulled out a chair from the table and sat down next to her. *I know I messed up, but just give me a chance to apologize, he thought. I won't ever repeat those past mistakes. I don't even know why I did what I did. I don't know if it's because of how I was raised, what my friends would think, revenge, or because I might like you. I don't know!* Rolling her eyes, Nell rapidly attempted to gather her books, but Paul moved his chair closer to hers and grabbed her hand.

"Don't say or do anything," Paul whispered. He moved his chair closer and locked their hands with his firm grip.

"What are you doing?" Nell demanded, trying to free herself.

"Shut up," he whispered. He glanced around the empty section of the library. "I know you hate me, but I don't hate you like my cousin or my girlfriend. I'm not really a jerk."

"Yeah right," Nell said. "Then why are you always treating me like crap? Why are you grabbing my hand like you are holding me hostage?"

"I don't have a choice," Paul whispered. "It's not like I can act like I did when we were alone at Sal's. You have no idea how dangerous that is."

"What are you talking about?"

"I can't be nice to you in public. My friends and family don't like colored people."

"Well, that's fine by me. I don't like white people."

"Cut the crap. If that were true, you wouldn't have brought me the pound cake."

"I only did it to say thanks, nothing more. I hate you!"

"I figured as much."

Paul let go of Nell's hand. He was done! Paul was defeated; he wanted to make amends, but she hated him, and he didn't blame her. He was the one who had wronged her, and he would have to live with his guilt. If he left then and there, at least he could distract himself by practicing football with the rest of the football team. One thing was for certain, he never wanted to relive that moment that he had experienced inside of Nell's car. He pushed his chair away from the table. Rising to his feet, he was ready to leave when he felt Nell's hand grab his.

"I'm sorry," she said.

Paul stood there for a moment and sat back down. He kept his eyes glued to the table. *Darn!* It was as if the roles of vulnerabilities were being exchanged. Paul took a deep breath to say what had been plaguing him since that horrible moment.

"I'm sorry too," he said. "I don't hate colored people, but I can't be nice to them either. If my family ever found out, it would be the end of me. I didn't want to kick your pencil away or toss your tray away. I know you won't believe a word of this, but I really wanted to eat your pound cake, but I couldn't, not with my girlfriend or cousin around. It was awfully hard for me to act that way. If I could be nice to you openly, I would be."

"Then, how is it that you can be with me like this in the library?"

"We could be partners for a class project; nobody would question that. Everyone knows we take some of the same classes."

"Then why did you grab my hand?"

"Do we really have to go into that?"

"Yeah, why?"

"So, you wouldn't be scared and run away."

"Well, you've been acting weird and make me uncomfortable."

She is right, Paul thought. I've done everything possible for her to mistrust me, and yet, she still is talking to me. I don't know much about colored people other than what I've been taught by my family and the media. She doesn't seem to be a bad person...Maybe, I could... see for myself what she is really like and learn a little bit more about the colored people to see for myself how they are...Also, maybe I could make amends.

"I apologize," Paul said. "I just didn't want you to leave before asking if I could spend time alone with you and learn more about you. I've never gotten a chance to spend a lot of time with a colored person before outside of class. I've always been taught to hate them, but you didn't seem to be a horrible person. I'm sorry for how I treated you, but I have a lot of eyes on me, and I have to act a certain way, otherwise I would get in trouble. I don't mean to creep you out or upset you."

"That sounds weird."

"It's not too much to ask for considering I changed your tire for free in the middle of a storm."

"You're not going to try to do anything else, are you?"

"No, I only wanted to spend time with you. I guess, I only held your hand at first because I didn't want you to run away from me, but the longer I held it, I just didn't want to let go."

Nell stared at him. Paul prayed that she would at least be open to the idea so that he could make amends. He never wanted to ever become that evil, wicked person who mistreated her before ever again. Even if she decided to never speak to him ever again, he would be content to know that she forgave him enough to listen to him that day.

"I'll spend time with you," Nell said. "But if you continue to humiliate me, I don't want to have anything more to do with you. First, I need to finish my homework."

"I promise that I won't ever do that again," Paul pledged.

Nell, then, offered her hand to him. Paul held onto it, under the table. Paul couldn't believe it! Never in his life had he imagined spending alone time with a Negro person, much less holding hands with one. Everyone that he knew would never have approved of such a scandalous scene, but yet, as small as it was, it did not seem as horrible as he had imagined and taught by others. Nell's hand was just as soft and warm as Nancy's. She seemed to be more focused on her math assignment than plotting any kind of malice acts against anyone. Paul studied her as she took her pencil and erased the answers to a math formula that she was obviously struggling. Paul waited to see, if she would ask him to do her work for her; but instead, she kept on erasing and changing her answers, opting to do things on her own. Paul peered at the math problem that was causing her to struggle.

"Didn't we go over that in class?" he asked. "It's pretty easy. I thought everyone in class understood it. Nobody asked any questions when the teacher was going over it today."

"To be honest, I don't understand any of the math we discussed in class," Nell said. "I wanted to ask questions, but the last time I did, people embarrassed me. I just don't want to look dumb in front of everyone. It's bad enough I am failing. It also doesn't help that I can't see the board, sitting all the way in the back of the classroom."

"Well, the way he explains it, it's harder than it has to be," Paul said. "You can do it a different way and still come up with the same correct answer." With his free hand, he grabbed a pencil and started to explain a different way to solve the math problem. Nell's eyes lit up. She understood how to follow the different way to solve the equation. It was less confusing and easier to follow. She wanted to cry, only this time, had tears of joy because she didn't feel confused anymore. To help her, Paul would give her different problem to solve and help her understand how to get the correct answers.

"How are you so good with math?" Nell asked. "I never would have guessed that someone like you...Sorry, I didn't mean..."

"What?" Paul said. "Just because I'm good at sports, I can't be good at other things? My family owns a store. We do math all the time and since I'm going to inherit it one day, I have to know how to make profits. What about your family? What do they do?"

"Not much," Nell said, "My mother cleans houses and my father used to work for this Negro company, until they left town. Now, he does odd jobs around town, hoping to find something permanent. I was working at the drive-in to help out, but lost my job... It's getting late, I better get home. I appreciate your help and staying around this late at the library to assist me. It's amazing that I can actually understand things now. You're a good teacher—no, a great teacher. I don't feel so bad about the class as much as I used to. I'm going to keep practicing once I get home. Thanks."

Paul and Nell walked out into the empty parking lot. Paul stayed about a yard away from her, hoping to indicate that he had no plans to harass her near her car. Nell climbed in and closed the creaky, old door.

"Nell," Paul said. "I'm sorry about you losing your job. I will talk to your boss and see if he will let you go back."

"I don't think so," said Nell, "not with your cousin going there. I'm sure that I will be able to find another job soon. If I was able to get that one, there will be others."

"Don't get me started on Bill. He's always been an asshole."

"Yeah, nobody likes him," Nell laughed.

"Will you be back at the library tomorrow?"

"I guess, why?"

"I'll see you there tomorrow after school then."

"Why? Don't you have other things to do?"

"Yeah, this is one of them."

"You're funny, Paul. I'll see you around."

Nell drove away, unaware of how serious Paul was about returning to the library. He enjoyed spending time with her and in a way, wanted more. As quiet and timid as Nell was, Paul questioned if she would ever attend any of the events at school, but then, he remembered how the other students didn't want people like her to attend. *Darn!* The only thing he could do with her was spend time after school at the library, but he had football practice too. *I forgot about practice again!* Then, all of his other free time was busy working at the family store and they played no games when it came to everyone pulling their weight. Paul would need to come up with a new plan, if he wanted to spend more time with Nell. He could always tell the coach that he would be a few minutes late because he was being tutored or tutoring another student. Heck, a few of the guys used that same excuse to spend more time with their girlfriends to sneak away and have sex, so why couldn't he use the same excuse? Spending a little bit of time with Nell would be better than none and he was going to seize the opportunity.

Paul hurried to the football field where the rest of the team was still practicing.

"Where have you been Boudreaux?" Coach Anderson asked.

"Sorry, Coach," Paul said. "I lost track of time."

"Hurry and get changed," Coach Anderson responded. "Two laps around the field. Be late for practice again and you're going to warm the benches next game!"

Chapter 6

Paul began dozing off during English class the next school day. He did not sleep well last night; his body was sore after running two laps around the football field and doing his duties at Sal's. He called the hospital to check on the status of his grandfather's condition and learned that it was getting slightly better, but not well enough to return home. Paul planned on visiting him that Saturday before returning to work. The other family members who worked in the store, which were mainly his cousins and uncle, detested working at Sal's. Often, Paul's family would complain that the store was taking over their lives due to Abraham's strict rules. The only day of rest was Sunday and Sunday always seemed so far away.

Paul's eyes were centimeters from closing when the bell rang, ending the school day. Someone let out a soft yawn, indicating that Paul wasn't the only person drowsy during the class.

"Don't forget to read chapters six and seven," Mrs. Miller, the English teacher, reminded the class, placing her book on her desk.

"You better show up early for practice today," Henry told Paul. "Coach has already been talking to Michael Favre. If you're benched, he could be quarterback for the next game."

"I told coach that I was going to be there, and I will," Paul sighed, grabbing his books from his desk. He yawned and pushed through the sea of students that crowded the hallway. He put his books away into his locker and headed to the library. Afterall, he still had another appointment. He opened the door to the library and walked in. The librarian was busy assisting another student in the area that had the card catalogues. Paul took his finger and dragged it across several books, pretending he was searching for a book. He heard the sound of the library door opening and closing. There were footsteps in the next aisle and Paul saw a figure moving down the aisle towards the back of the library. Paul quickly began to follow the figure to the back, spotting Nell and watching her sit down in her usual hiding spot. Smirking, Paul pulled out the chair next to her and sat down.

"So, you were serious about coming," Nell said. She opened one of her books and began scanning it with her eyes.

"Yeah, but only for a few minutes; I have practice."

"If your busy, you don't have to be here."

"I *want* to be here," Paul said. "As I said before, I wanted to learn more about you."

"There's not much to say, so I don't know what it is that you are trying to learn."

"How about this...What were things like at Freedmen's High School? I've seen it, but never went there. Tell me something about your time there."

"As you know, our building was pretty old," said Nell, "but it was all that we had, and we tried to maintain it the best way that we could. Our school didn't get as much money or resources as Wood Oak High School. Everything was used and recycled. We never got new textbooks. We received the discarded textbooks from Wood Oak High School. You'd be lucky to get a book that had *all* the pages because by the time we got the used books five or six people had used it before we did. Sometimes the books would have writings or notes in them. I didn't mind that because sometimes the notes would be helpful. I am grateful for what I learned from my teachers who worked there. They did their best to provide us with the best possible education that they could give us. My grandparents couldn't read or write, just like the generations before them. My parents have some education, but they had to leave school to work and provide for me and my siblings. If things go well, I will be the first person in my family to graduate from high school. That's why it's important for me to do well. I have to set a good example for my sister and brother. In my community, our reputation is everything; that's why you often hear people asking who you are related to or who you are associated with."

Paul thought about Nell's response. Ever since he could remember, most of everything that he had obtained had been brand new. Wood Oak High School wasn't a brand-new school, but most of what was inside was new including the books, science labs, and any other materials needed for class. Most of the teens at Wood Oak High had taken their books for granted and thought nothing of trying to preserve them for the next set of hands that would receive them, even though it was encouraged by teachers to take care of the books. As far as Paul knew, most of the people in his family had always managed to go to school and finish.

"What do you do for fun, Nell?" asked Paul, hoping to lighten up the mood.

"My family and I go to the Negro church," Nell replied. "There, we have services, picnics, and other gatherings in our community. On Sundays, we have services at 8 a.m., 12 p.m., and 6 p.m. We used to have sporting events after school, but I'm not knowledgeable about sports and would just talk to my friends when we sat in the bleachers. Also, I like to help my mother with the cooking. We usually prepare food for the week together in the kitchen, so that when we all return home, there is always something to eat. My family likes eating fish, sweet peas, mustard greens, gumbo, and cabbage. I like listening to the music on the radio. I listen to everything, but I have two left feet. What do you do for fun? I already know you like sports, but I'm sure you like other things."

"I like music too, especially rock and roll," said Paul. "My favorite television program is American Bandstand. They play music and everyone gets to see people participate in dancing competitions. Sometimes, I wish that I could get on that show myself because I like dancing!"

"*You* dance?" Nell chuckled.

"Yeah!"

"You're pulling my leg, Paul!"

"Honest! You can ask anyone here!"

"I have to see that to believe it!"

"I'll show you one day!" Paul promised. He peered at the clock above them. It was time to go. Paul said his goodbyes and headed out to the field, reminiscing about their short time together. He joined the rest of the football team, while planning his next visit to the library.

Chapter 7

Henry brought the cigarette to his lips and inhaled. Paul and the other two football players began to cough. It was a new school day and the guys had gathered in Henry's car to listen to the music on the radio before school started.

"Can't you go one day without smoking?" a football player named Daniel Harris asked.

"My car, my smokes," Henry replied.

"Did you guys hear about what happened to Pricilla Jenkins last Saturday?" Steven Quimby, another football player, stated. "She was driving around town with those orange juice cans in her hair, and she was so mad!"

"Didn't she have a date with Frank?" Paul asked.

"Yeah, but he got caught cheating," Steven laughed. "We all were supposed to have our double date at Earl's and you know Pricilla, she was trying to contact him an hour before the date and his mother told Pricilla that he was already on his date! Pricilla was so mad that she called some of her friends and found out that he was at the bowling alley with this other girl. I heard she stormed into the building and got him good!"

It was minutes before the bell would ring. Henry turned the car radio off and put out his cigarette. All four teens left the car to be met by Nancy and a few of her cheerleader friends at the entrance of the school. Nancy gave Paul a quick smooch on the lips and the bell rang, starting the new school day. After gathering their books, the teens assembled into their homeroom classroom. Paul's eyes widened when he realized that he had forgotten to read the last chapter in the book for his English class. He was so tired that night, he only read one chapter and had planned on reading the last chapter that morning. Swearing under his breath, Paul took out his book and began to read. His eyes quickly read through the first paragraph when *it* happened. Paul got a quick whiff of that same beautiful, alluring floral scent. He gazed from his book as Nell made her way to the back of the classroom. Paul pressed his lips together to hide his smile. *Every day, she smells nice.* He continued to read until it was time to leave for math class.

During math class, Mr. Thomas introduced a new math formula and had several students go to the board to complete several math equations. Of course, Henry was called to the board, along with three other students. After they displayed their answers, Mr. Thomas reviewed them with the class, until he came near Henry. The teacher's nostrils began to flare as he sniffed.

"Do I smell smoke?" he asked. He turned to Henry who looked stone faced. "Henry, why do I smell smoke on you?"

"My parents smoke and sometimes it gets on my clothes," Henry said.

The class waited in anticipation for the teacher's response. Paul grimaced. He knew that Henry had been truthful in saying that his parents smoked, and it did get on his clothes. However, Henry also smoked and would sometimes steal a cigarette or two from his father's stash to later smoke whenever he had the chance. In fact, Paul wondered why it had taken so long for any adult to notice that the teen had been smoking at school.

"I see," Mr. Thomas said lowering his glasses. He studied Henry's calm stance before moving back to his desk and facing the board again. "Your answer is correct Henry. Take a seat."

Henry shot a quick smirk at Paul and strolled back to his seat. Mr. Thomas called three more students to the board, including Nell *and* Bill. Paul watched carefully as Nell began to write her answer on the board. During it all, Paul spotted an error. He wanted to tell her but knew that he couldn't. Nobody was allowed to correct another student's work on the board except Mr. Thomas. Mr. Thomas began with the first student, whose answer was correct. Then Mr. Thomas began with Bill's whose was incorrect. Mr. Thomas began to go over the correct answer.

Come on, Nell, Paul thought. You forgot to subtract the last part of the equation!

Paul covered his face partially as Mr. Thomas went down to Nell's work. Nell looked over her problem and soon spotted her own error, correcting it. Mr. Thomas studied her answer and to Paul's surprise Mr. Thomas responded that the answer was incorrect. Confused, Paul listened as the teacher explained the reasoning behind the answer.

I don't get it, Paul thought. I thought that it went strictly as it did the last time! Nell smiled at the teacher, accepting the answer. She went back to her seat, but Paul raised his hand, asking for a further explanation. Mr. Thomas explained it in the same manner in which he explained it before, confusing Paul. For the remainder of class, whenever the teacher would call upon other students, it was as if the answers were worked as before, at least, minus Nell's equation.

"I guess you won't be smoking in the mornings anymore," Steven said to Henry, who rolled his eyes, at the end of class.

"If Mr. Thomas believed me that time, why wouldn't he the second time?" Henry said, "Least I just smoke cigs; other badasses smoke weed."

"I used to smoke cigarettes," Paul confessed. "When my father was alive, he used to smoke all the time. I would just wait for him to toss away his cigarettes and when he left, I'd just pick it up and smoke it. I didn't quit until he did."

"How are you two guys even able to run with all that smoking?" Daniel asked.

"I quit years ago," Paul said. "I haven't smoked since I was ten."

"Both of my parents smoke," Henry said. "I used to do what Paul did when I was little; just get 'em off my parents. Now, I just get some from their packs when they just leave them around the house. They don't count what's in the pack."

All four guys pushed their way through the crowd of students, each one parting ways into a different classroom. Paul thought about his father, Andrew Boudreaux, a man who was in his late thirties during that time. He always had a charming smile on his face, but could be strict, during certain times. As far as Paul could remember, his father had always been kind-hearted towards him, his mother, and his grandfather. In fact, both his father and grandfather got along so well that even though his grandfather had two other sons, Paul's father was clearly the favorite. Paul's uncle who was also Bill's father, Harry Boudreaux, was the complete opposite. Like Bill, he always had a scowl on his face and mistreated his wife and son, including his nephew, Wally, who was now twenty-four years old and still living with him. Wally had been adopted by Harry years ago and had been declared as his other "son." Bill had an older sister named Linda, who was now twenty years old, but she moved out to attend nursing school in another parish. Bill's family lived across the street from Paul, who was living with his grandfather in his grandfather's house. Often, there would be screams and the sound of items shattering coming from the house across the street, making Paul wish that he never heard such atrocities. It was no wonder that Bill did not turn out any worse than he already was. *Maybe he fights everyone because he cannot fight his father, Paul thought, viewing Bill in the science classroom.*

"Bill is Harry's son," Abraham told Paul years ago. "What goes on in Harry's house is his own business."

Chapter 8

"Why are you always looking down?" Paul asked Nell one day in the library. "Don't you know that you are making yourself look uptight? If you held your head up high, people wouldn't target you as much."

"Easy for you to say," Nell said. "You don't get picked on every day. I keep my eyes low so that I don't cry in front of these horrible people. I have no friends here at this school. The people who I was friends with at my other school aren't here with me. At least they were smart enough to go to the other Negro school far away from here. I didn't even want to go to Wood Oak High School, but it was closer to where I lived, and my parents had this awful notion that maybe things would have changed here."

Paul leaned forward in his chair. In a way, he understood what it was like to be alone and lonely. When he was not at school, on a date, or at work, he would be at home in his grandfather's house, alone. The interior of the house had all the latest, modern furniture. Unlike many homes, his grandfather's five-bedroom house had a colored television, washer and dryer, rotary phone, record player (with many records), comfortable sofas, and chairs in rooms with vibrant colors and patterns. As beautiful as the home was, without his grandfather, Paul lived there by himself. For weeks, Paul had managed to keep himself busy, but once all tasks were completed, he had no family to go home to and the family that he did have across the street despised him.

"I could be your friend, Nell," Paul offered.

"Thanks, but I can make it on my own," Nell said.

"No, really, I will be."

"Why? We have nothing in common."

"You want friends and I want to be yours. Plus, we do have something in common: our love of music."

Paul waited for her answer, but Nell only began to fidget before rubbing her arms. She closed her eyes briefly and let out a deep exhale. Disappointed, Paul rubbed the back of his neck with his hand and hunched forward.

"I have to go, Nell," said Paul. "I have football practice. I will see you tomorrow." He exhaled deeply as he left the library to go back to the field to be with the team. He was unhappy that there had been no response to his offer, but he was not shocked. He had yearned for a chance, but the ball was in Nell's court if she would allow any type of friendship between them. Before then, Paul seldomly had to ask for friendships. People always came to him, the popular teen. He had accepted most, but things were different with her, Nell. He wanted her friendship, and possibly more.

"Where have you been?" Henry asked when he spotted Paul on the field.

"Getting tutoring," Paul said.

"Really? I thought your grades were good."

"Only because I am trying to keep it that way."

After practice and work, Paul was drained. He drove himself home to the empty house that he shared with his grandfather. Inside, he didn't bother to look at the many eyes gawking at him from old family photos that hung from the wall, for he knew they all would now hate him. He closed the door behind himself and scurred up the stairs to his bedroom. His muscles ached and pulsated greater once he collapsed onto his bed. He waited to change his clothes. He didn't want to open the door to one of his secrets. It never had been *his* originally anyway, but it was his fate. But was it? Paul closed his eyes momentarily, imagining how far he had fallen away from his family tree. None of them would ever possibly accept him again, and still, he was the next in line. Paul swallowed hard and rose from his bed. He opened up the closet door within his room, pushing back the white regalia that was pictured within so many pictures of his family's album. His grandfather had given it to him in advance for his future advanced initiation on his eighteenth birthday. In the back of Paul's closet was a chest that he pulled out. Inside the chest, there was a great red book entitled, The Album. He shuttered to think of the ill-fated memorabilia that was shown inside. Clutching the album and white regalia, he carried them to the room down the hallway, two rooms away, into his grandfather's room. Paul opened the door and placed the items onto his grandfather's bed.

"I can't do this anymore," Paul said, his voice cracking. He walked out the room and closed the door behind himself. He went back to his room and gazed out the window, viewing his aunt, Henrietta Boudreaux, who was sitting out on the porch near a porch light. Her distraught face hung low, gazing at her old worn sold blue dress that had a small rip near the sleeve. Barely noticeable, Paul could make out the discoloration of the black and blue mark around her arm. Henrietta was Bill's mother, and it was surprising that she was finally being allowed to go back outside, especially after what had occurred that ill-fated day years ago when a Negro man was caught alone with her in the house. Paul's uncle, Harry Boudreaux, caught them and shot the man dead in the front yard.

"H-he raped me!" Henrietta exclaimed to her husband when she was questioned why the man was there. Paul knew that was a lie. He had seen the man at the house many times when his uncle and cousins were away; it was just that one time, they were caught. Paul could only watch from his window as the man was shot dead by his uncle in a fit of rage while trying to escape from the house.

"That'll teach you," Harry shouted, spitting on the ground where the man lay dead. Then, holding the gun pointed at Henrietta, he continued, "You allowed him to touch you, didn't you? You fuckin' whore! I should shoot you dead too!"

Henrietta tried to hold up her arms defensively, but her husband struck her down too with the back of his fists. Turning back to the body of the Negro man, Harry shot more rounds from his gun until the barrels of his gun were empty. Crowds of neighbors began to form before the police were summoned.

Chapter 9

During halftime, Paul lingered by the fence. He spotted a few recognizable faces from his classes and their parents. The only family that he had there was Bill, and he was busy gorging down hotdogs and soda, gawking at Nancy. Nancy paid Bill no attention as her affections fell upon Paul. She gave him a quick wink before continuing the cheer routine. Paul obliged with a smile, but soon sulked. Every one of his usual friends was there, happy and cheerful, but the one person that he wanted to see there wasn't. He wasn't stunned but was still saddened. He didn't blame her for not responding to his requests for some sort of friendship. Often, Paul would wish that he could go back in time and change his actions. However, once reality set back in and knowing that there was nothing more that he could do, Paul had no choice but to move on. All his life he had been taught that *his* people came first and foremost and how much his people had become invisible. Maybe Nell felt the same way about *her* people. Who was Paul to blame her for her beliefs when he was taught and believed the same at one point? *However, Paul thought, it would have been nice if, maybe, she would have thought about me as often as I thought about her.* Grumbling to himself, Paul tightened his grip to his helmet thinking how foolish he was to have ever entertained such an idea. He still had his memories of spending time with her, and it had been pleasant and informative. He learned about her old school, how she wanted to be successful in life, and how she had persevered through many obstacles.

When it was time to return to the field, Paul cleared his throat and began to refocus on the game again. His team needed him, and Paul was desperate for a distraction. With the football now in his hands, Paul threw the ball to the end. Unfortunately, another member of the opposing team intercepted the ball. The crowd from the opposing team cheered wildly as the player began to run towards the other end of the field. Several members of Paul's team took after the person with the ball. Luckily, Henry caught the person, bringing him down before he was able to make a touchdown.

"Get your head in the game Boudreaux," Coach Anderson bellowed to Paul.

The opposing team took over the ball and they started their drive to Paul's teams' goal line. The opposing quarterback ran four plays, and the opposing team scored a touchdown. The crowd of the opposing team cheered. Angry, the fans of the Wood Oak High Tigers began to complain and booed the other team. After the touchdown and the extra point, the opposing team kicked off to the Wood Oak High Tigers and they returned it to the thirty-yard line. Then Paul came out as quarterback again, this time hoping for better results. Paul took the snap from the center and handed the ball off to the fullback who gained seven yards. On the next play, Paul took the ball and passed it to his wide receiver who caught the ball for thirty yards. On the next play, Paul threw the ball to the tight end who grabbed it and ran to the goal line, scoring a touchdown.

At the end of the game, Paul's team won with the final score 21 to 14. The Wood Oak High Tiger fans cheered and began congratulating the team. Excited, Paul and the rest of the team began goofing around about the plays, until Paul made out a lone figure in the parking lot watching them. Squinting his eyes, Paul spotted Nell standing by herself. Elated, Paul shouted louder, pumping a fist into the air.

Chapter 10

Fuming, Paul bit into his pasta as he glanced across the cafeteria. Today, Nell had company at her table. Martin was sitting next to her, eating peas from his tray of food. *Where did he come from and why is he sitting there?* Fury and jealousy began to brew within Paul the longer Martin lounged next to Nell. Martin usually never stayed in the cafeteria long, but out of all the places he could sit, he chose to sit next to the person Paul began to secretly claim for himself. Sure, Paul had Nancy as his girlfriend, but he also liked Nell and whether she and the school knew it or not, he had staked a claim on her internally. He speculated if Martin had asked Nell out and if that was the reason why he was there. *Just because they are the same race didn't mean that only Martin should be Nell's choice! What about me? I liked her long before he did! Sure, she is colored and I'm white, but that doesn't mean that I shouldn't be allowed to be with a fox like her! I'd give anything to sit at that table! This is unreal!*

"It was like that guy came out of nowhere," Henry said, at the table where the popular kids sat. "I thought that Steven was going to catch the ball and then before I knew it, the ball was heading to the other end of the field!"

"He caught us all off guard," Daniel said. "We just couldn't catch him. He ran like a bat out of Hell!"

"I still caught him," Henry boasted. "*Maybe* I was just a *little bit* faster."

"Have you seen Mrs. Brody?" Steven asked. "She sure is foxy."

"I don't have her, but I sure wish I did," Daniel replied. "My teacher for English is the old battle axe, Mrs. Miller. I wish I had Mrs. Brody. Too bad she is married."

"What you expect her to do, wait until you graduate to sign your yearbook and marry you?" Paul joked, refocusing back to the conversation that was occurring at his own table.

"I'd marry her," Steven replied.

"Don't let Kristy hear you say that," Henry warned him, stuffing his mouth with the last remnants of pasta. "She can get worse than Pricilla and you heard what Pricilla did to Frank when she got to the bowling alley."

"I'm not going steady with Kristy," Steven retorted. "She wants me to go steady with her, but I'm not. Frank's mistake was going steady with Pricilla and then changing his mind later. I warned him not to do that. His ring had probably been on every girl's finger by now."

"What grade do you have in Mrs. Brody's class, Steven?" Henry asked.

"Straight As," said Steven. "Besides being sexy, she is a good teacher."

Grabbing their trays, the guys emptied them and gave it back to the cafeteria staff. Now in the hallway, they began to goof off, hollering in the process until one of the nearby teachers instructed for them to quiet down. Turning the corner of the hallway, they moved near the trophy case where many trophies were from years past. Wood Oak High School had awards for track and field, baseball, and football. Most of the trophies for the football team had been from when the school had placed first in their district, and second in regionals. The only time the team never placed was the time Freddy Kleinpeter was quarterback for the first few games until his grades got bad and he was removed from the team, resulting in the team having a losing season in 1965. Also included in the trophy case were academic achievement awards for science fairs, English compositions, spelling bees, and much more.

Crash! Boom! Down the 12th grade hallway, Bill shoved another student into the lockers as he continued his stroll down the hallway. Bill panted as he walked, breathing with his mouth open. Papers and books scattered to the ground away from the other student's arms; Bill kicked them across the floor, clearing his path.

"Get out of my way, you dumbass," he said.

Outraged, the other student grabbed his book and hurled it at Bill, hitting the back of his head. Bill turned around and began chasing the student down the hallway, but soon stopped, running out of breath. Paul grabbed the bridge of his nose and scowled. He was ashamed to call Bill his relative. He always brought negative attention towards himself, only being polite towards Nancy and rarely others. Paul tried to avoid Bill as much as possible but said nothing if Bill happened to wander within his circle of friends. Bill certainly had nowhere else to go or do. He had no friends of his own, except for Nancy who would force a smile at him in his face, pretending to be friendly. However, once Bill would leave, she would talk bad about him behind his back saying how gross he was.

"He is just so disgusting," Nancy would say within the circle of popular teens. *"He sweats all the time, and he makes this annoying sound when he breathes through his mouth."*

"Why can't you just tell him to go away, Nancy?" one of the cheerleaders asked Nancy.

"Then how would that make me look if he were to offend me in front of everyone?" Nancy snorted. *"I will not be humiliated in front of the school by the likes of that sweaty neanderthal. I'd rather just hang tough."*

"I just want to pound him right now," Henry muttered balling his fist and punching it into the palm of his other hand.

"Just tune him out," Paul suggested. *"Long as we are all on his good side, he's harmless."*

"I don't like him, Paul," Nancy said. *"I wish you would do or say something to make him flake off."*

"I can't do anything; he's my cousin," Paul replied.

"If he weren't, the team and I would have let him have it," Henry said.

"He gets enough of that at home, just let him be," Paul sighed.

In a way, Paul could see why Bill became the way that he was. Bill's father, Harry Boudreaux, mistreated his own wife, Henrietta Boudreaux, and beat her daily. He was a trigger happy, miserable soul who was just angry at the world for unknown reasons, other than everyone knowing that his wife often had affairs inside their marriage. He often made his wife stay home, like a caged animal, while he was at work at the family store. Bill's sister, Linda, and their cousin, Wally, who also lived in the same household often kept tight lipped about everything, but the family knew everything, especially since the police was often called onto the property. Everything, however, was often swept under the rug because they had distant family and associates within the police department.

"If she kept her legs closed, he wouldn't beat her as much," Paul's grandfather, Abraham, said one day during dinner before his hospitalization. *"I never liked that wide legged whore, and I don't see why he doesn't just get rid of her and get it over with. Harry should have just married a decent woman like your father did. Andrew never had any problems with Helen. At least with Andrew I can say that I had one decent son out of the three. Your Uncle Harry can't even go one month without asking me for money, and he wonders why I'm not leaving him the store or the cabin. If he can't keep his own finances and house in order, why should I leave him anything? Your father, Paul, now he kept things in order and had a good head on his shoulders. We were making profits and he was well respected. That's why you're living here and not with that idiot across the street. I need to have at least one heir that isn't a disappointment."*

"What about Wally?" Paul asked.

"I don't trust that sneaky bastard," Abraham muttered. *"I caught him trying to steal from me once and that was all it took for me to lose all respect for him. If he stole from me, he would steal from you, remember that if he ever comes crawling to you for a handout or sympathy. His parents were a piece of garbage too. His mother was the biggest gossip in town and his father tried to rape your mother. I got sick of them both; that's*

why his father ended up in The Album. Wally's probably still bitter about it, but if he tries anything, he knows there is a fresh bullet waiting for his head."

During English class, the students took turns reading out loud while others listened. Henry brought his book closer to his face. In between the pages of his book was a car magazine. He gasped at the picture of the new car model with the sparkling metallic engine.

"Oh, yeah," he breathed.

"Henry!" Mrs. Miller said. "Read the next page."

Henry tensed and began flipping his book back to the pages that the class was reading.

"Page 128," Paul murmured.

Henry quickly began to flip to the page, but Mrs. Miller was now standing next to him. She held out her hand and waited. Henry grumbled and handed the teacher the magazine. Mrs. Miller tossed the magazine on top of her desk and went back to Henry.

"Page 128," she said sternly. She stood next to him while he read the page. Once Henry had completed the task, Mrs. Miller leaned forward and whispered to him. "This is the third time you got caught with a magazine in class. Thirty minutes detention."

Henry tossed his head back and tilted forward. He was going to miss part of football practice and Coach Anderson would make him run the field and do pushups.

"You should have known better," Paul muttered when the bell rang. "You're always doing these crazy stunts to get yourself in trouble."

"That story was boring, and I had to do something to keep myself awake," Henry murmured.

"I'll see you on the field," Paul said, heading out the door. He saw that Nancy was standing near his locker. With a big smile, she greeted him with a quick kiss on the lips.

"Kristy and I were going to have a get together after the game on Friday at my house," she said. "I wanted to see if you and Henry would come over so we all could listen to some new 45 records and have some fun."

"Sure," said Paul. "Sounds like we all will have a blast. I'll tell Henry and bring some records over."

Nancy squealed with delight and gave him another smooch before departing. Almost skipping, she giggled when she approached her friends. The girls waved and winked at Paul before they exited the building, making Paul blush. He stuffed his books into his locker and hastened his walk to the other end of the school, ending where the library door was open. He nodded at the librarian who was busy reading a book behind the counter. Paul scanned the library, as usual it was quiet and peaceful. He met Nell at the back of the library. His lips curled into a smile when he noticed that this time, she was gazing at him with a slight smile. Satisfied and glowing internally, Paul rested next to her.

"I saw you at the game," Paul said. "Did you show up to watch the game or just to see *me*?" He waited for her to tell him how great he was and how much she wanted him, like all the other girls had done before. But the words never came, surprising him.

Nell's smile faded.

Oh, no, Paul thought. I'm coming across as an arrogant jerk. I better fix this!

"Thanks for showing up, Nell," he said. "Out of everyone that was there, you're the one I wanted to see the most."

"Congratulations on your win," Nell said. "I wanted to go inside to watch, but it didn't seem like a good idea and Bill was there. So, I watched behind the fence...Today, in my home economics class, we learned how to make tea cakes and I saved some for you. It was my first time making them; I hope you like them." She opened her purse and pulled out a white handkerchief with three small tea cakes wrapped inside. She handed the gift to Paul, who was speechless. "I made the handkerchief too. It was one of the first projects I made at Freedmen's High School before coming here. I was saving it for a special occasion and your win was special."

Humbled, Paul tilted his head forward and began blinking quickly to stop himself from crying. He couldn't remember the last time someone had made something from scratch for him. He carefully unwrapped the tea cakes and handed one to Nell.

"Thank you, Nell," he said. "For giving me another special occasion to celebrate." He bit into one of the tea cakes and it tasted just as beautiful as that moment between them.

Chapter 11

Later that day at Sal's, Harry Boudreaux slammed his fists against the counter causing it to shake. His face was unshaven, showing particles of grey and black hairs on his jaw and chin. His eyes were red from the lack of sleep he had been having for the past two days. Inches away from him was his cane leaning against the back of the counter. His red and white plaid shirt had overalls attached to his solid black pants. He tossed the paper on the counter. A new store was opening in Wood Oak, meaning more competition against Sal's Country Store. Last month, they had a 30% loss from their usual profit. It didn't help that the family already had a bad enough reputation around town due to their negative history and questionable activities. Once upon a time, the family had managed to successfully do away with competitors by staging "accidents" but that changed drastically since Abraham's hospitalization. Abraham knew how to get rid of problems, but due to his ill health, he had not called anymore hits on anyone. Instead, he blamed Harry and his sons for their damaging standings within the community.

"New store to bring the community together? Over my dead body!" Harry croaked with his frog like voice. "Where's my advertisement? Bill, didn't Wally place that ad in the paper as I asked him to?"

"He said he did," stated Bill.

"Then why don't I see it in the paper?" Harry shouted, balling up his newspaper. He stormed into the back of the store and slammed the door behind himself.

"What a *disgusting* man," a female customer muttered as Paul picked up her bags to help her to her car.

Harry's angry outburst was becoming a regular thing at the store, embarrassing the family more than ever. When Abraham was actively running the store, things were calmer and organized, peaceful for the most part. Since his hospitalization, Abraham reluctantly had Harry manage the store in his absence, but the store was suffering under his mismanagement, mainly due to his abuse of his employees, which were his own family members. Wally, who helped to manage the store during the day, was old enough to manage the store better than Harry and was more successful, but money often disappeared under him. Abraham had verbalized that he wanted Paul to take over operations, but Paul was still in high school and was unable to keep a close enough watchful eye on the store. All he could do was phone his grandfather and be honest about how the store was being run, making Abraham even more furious at the rest of the family.

Paul managed to help a few more customers when Wally came back to the store, returning from his break. Wally, thin, with a neatly trimmed beard and his family's signature black hair and grey eyes had a constant look of worry in his eyes. He had a solid white shirt and black pants with black overalls. He stepped behind the counter, unaware of Harry's new rampage. Irate, Harry stomped from the backroom, swearing at Wally in front of the remaining customers.

"You stole the money again, didn't you?" Harry shouted at Wally.

"No, Pop," Wally said.

"I called the newspaper and they denied ever receiving the money I gave you to give to them," Harry bellowed.

Uneasy, Wally continued to deny the accusations. He calmly asked Harry if he wanted to go into the backroom and discuss matters in private instead of in the presence of the customers. Harry agreed, but not before calling him as many swear words before closing the door behind them.

"I can't wait for that new store to open up," a customer whispered to Paul. "I hate coming here and seeing all of this tension. I hope you will go there too. You deserve to be in a better place than this."

"Thank you, sir," was all that Paul could say. Paul wanted to have nothing to do with the store. He still wanted to leave town and start his life anew. His grandfather had promised him a nice inheritance, should he pass. With that inheritance, Paul could live his dream of a new beginning. If the rest of the family wanted the store, they could have it, as far as Paul was concerned. Paul checked his watch; it was time for his break. He took off his apron, walked outside, and sat out on the bench. He leaned back and looked at the tranquil blue sky as the clouds slowly crept forward. The parking lot had fewer cars. More and more customers were beginning to drive a little further to the outskirts of town to purchase groceries and other items, decreasing profits. The few customers that remained loyal to Sal's Country Store were those who had children who attended Wood Oak High School with Paul, but even they were talking about the new store that was being built. Every day, there were ads about the new store's grand opening, which was just around the corner.

Whoosh! Slam! Bill had exited the store. He appeared irritated and rested at the far end of the bench.

"You got a phone call in the back," he told Paul.

Paul reentered the store and went to the back. He picked up the phone and answered. It was a phone call from Abraham.

"Paul, how are you?" Abraham asked, with a weak voice.

"I'm fine; how are you?"

"Could be better, but I am still hanging on. How are things at the store?"

"Could be better; The store is doing okay, but some of our regular customers are going to the store in Merrydale."

"Merrydale? That's a twenty-minute drive. I saw the ad in the paper for that new Reynold's Store. They have a lot of guts to be moving in on Boudreaux territory. Wood Oak is my town, and that family should know better. Everyone can talk all they want, but that store is not going to open. Not while I still have breath in me. Those other families can drive all the way to Merrydale all they want but Sal's will still be the major store in Wood Oak. I will personally see to that!"

Chapter 12

The Wood Oak Hospital was chilly and dreary. It was one of those rare days in which Paul could take off from his duties at Sal's. His grandfather had made a specific request to see the young man, not knowing when it would be his final day at life. The nurses in their uniforms moved about in the corridor like ghosts who haunted the grim facility. An elderly man lay in a wheelchair near a wall. His head was tilted forward and his mouth slightly open, allowing for a long string of droll to fall onto his already soaked shirt.

Turning the corridor, a nurse was comforting a sobbing woman. The woman was hysterical and had a tissue hanging from her hand. The nurse grasped onto the woman's body before it hit the ground. The nurse pulled the woman back up and both women resumed their walk. Paul tried his best to drown out the sounds of the woman's wails. He stopped in front of the room that his grandfather had been staying in. He knocked on the door, but there was no answer. Gradually pushing the door open, Paul entered the room. It had a single bed, window with a closed curtain, small black and white television, two chairs, and a private bathroom. In the bed, his grandfather was resting with his eyes closed. His chest rose and fell as he breathed. His hair was fully grey, and his once powerful physique was a mere shadow of what it once was. He now appeared more wrinkled and feeble.

Paul approached the bed and stood near Abraham. He did not look like his condition was improving in the slightest.

"Grandfather," Paul said.

The old man gave no response and remained asleep. Paul sat down in a nearby chair and waited.

This is a downer, Paul thought. After he is gone, I won't have anyone but my friends. What good is having what little shattered fragments of a family that I do have when none of them care if I was alive or dead? Grandfather lived his life to make sure we had the best and even after doing some morally questionable deeds, he was dissatisfied most of his life. He would even be upset with me if he knew everything. I still love and care about you, Grandfather, but I don't want to live a life full of regrets.

"Paul," the old man said softly.

Paul's eyes broadened. He approached the side of the bed where Abraham grasped his hand. It was cold and clammy. Paul could see the veins through the thin skin of his grandfather's hand. The icy grey from his eyes were almost statuesque.

"Do you need another blanket?" Paul asked.

"Yes."

Paul exited the room and got an extra blanket. He returned and carefully covered the elderly man with the blanket. He also partially pushed back the curtain to the window, making the room lighter. His grandfather covered his eyes marginally with his hands and sluggishly moved his hands away. There was a noticeable, slight shaking of Abraham's hands.

"You've always been a good boy, Paul," Abraham stated. "I've never had to discipline you once and could always trust you to do the right thing for the good of your people. Everything I've done, I've done it for you. I never wanted you to go through the hardships that I've experienced growing up. You've always been appreciative and worked vigorously for everything you've earned. I am so proud of you." He wiped a tear from his eye. "I know that I probably may not make it to see you graduate from high school, but always know that if I ever had any love for anyone in the end, it has been for you."

"I love you too, Grandfather," Paul said.

After he left the hospital, Paul lounged in his car. Regardless of any racial matters, things seemed to always be about survival with one group fighting for resources against another. It all seemed to be a pitiful game of winner takes all, no matter who suffered any casualties or varied losses. It had been a wretched game that had gone too far for far too long, regardless of race. Loving his grandfather and people did not mean that he would choose to continue to be an active participant in the downfall of another group of people. Whatever it meant to uplift *everyone* seemed to be a more logical and humanitarian way of solving issues.

Paul drove his car to the outskirts of Freedmen's Street, daring not to cross those lines. Beyond a few buildings and homes, he could see the remnants left of the old high school: burnt, splintered wood with traces of brick that were once used as steps. A few of the nearby homes ranged from shotgun houses made of wood and a few made of brick, but moderate in appearance. A person or two sat on the porches, fanning themselves with paper fans. Further down into the abyss of the street, Paul could barely make out small children engaged in games of hopscotch or chasing one another as an adult stood nearby.

Backing up his car, Paul drove away from the Negro community and entered into the poor white community. He stopped near the Wilkerson house that was also a wooden home with brick steps and saw Henry working on his vehicle. His brother and sisters were running in the front yard playing while their mother was cradling her youngest child on the porch. Farther down the street, was the middle-class neighborhood where Nancy's family lived. The Perkins owned a modest four-bedroom home that had a beautiful yard with a variety of flowers and a magnolia tree in the front yard and one in the back.

Continuing his drive, Paul drove between Bill's home and the house he shared with Abraham. Bill's house was also modest, but was made of brick and had a beautifully landscaped yard with many flowers and a small picket fence. Across the street was Paul's home, the beautifully landscaped five-bedroom house with the latest of everything. Paul pressed his foot on the gas pedal, ending his drive at Sal's.

Inside the store, he put on his apron and began he usual duties of stocking shelves, helping with inventory, and sweeping. Meanwhile, Bill, Wally, and Harry were in the midst of their usual disputes. Paul tuned out the noise, welcoming the peaceful memories of days past. He hummed a peaceful tune to himself, grabbing ahold of another canned item. He put it in the usual place, where the others were usually stacked and categorized. Grabbing another, he gazed at the can.

"Maybe," he said, "it's time to go somewhere different."

Paul glanced at an empty section on the shelf and placed it there instead. He grabbed the label and moved it as well. It would take some time for him to get used to putting the different canned items in a new place, but in his mind and heart, Paul welcomed the change.

Chapter 13

For the next few days, Paul thought long and hard about the people in his life, desiring to make the changes that he needed. He had no qualms about how others wanted to do things about their own, but he wanted to start being honest with himself, starting with his beliefs that nobody was better than the other, regardless of their money, status, or color. Although his grandfather was powerful and had plenty of money, he never had the happiness that he wanted. The rest of Paul's family wanted money and power, but if they could not find happiness within each other, how would money and power make a difference? Most of the people that he knew that were poverty stricken spent most of their time trying to survive, sometimes at the expense of their families, their health, their communities, or other things. Everyone had troubles.

Furthermore, Paul came to the realization that even though he cared for Nancy, he had only thought of her as a friend. He knew that she loved him, but Paul wanted to follow his heart and be with the girl that he would have no question about giving his ring to. Understandably, it seemed unfair to leave Nancy, but it would be more unethical to remain in a relationship that he did not see himself growing in, knowing that he wanted to be with someone else.

With his thoughts blooming with his final decision, Paul went to the library faithfully to be with the girl he wished to be with and the one who often occupied most of his thoughts, Nell. He enjoyed his time with her and found her to be the genuine, sensitive, and supportive person that he needed in his life. So far, they were only friends. Anxiously, one afternoon, Paul followed Nell to her car in the empty parking lot. No longer afraid of him, Nell opened the passenger door without hesitation. Pleased, Paul sat down next to her.

"What do you want, Paul?" Nell inquired.

"You already know what I want," he said.

"Well, you usually hold my hand in the library, but today you are back in my car. What do you want this time?"

"Tell me what *you* want," Paul countered. "You know our situation. It can stay the same or it can change. I want you to be honest with me. Would you ever consider seeing me as more than just a classmate or a friend?"

"I can't because you are already seeing Nancy," Nell said. "Plus, you said that your friends and family wouldn't agree, so what is there to talk about? It's not me, it's you."

Paul remained quiet for a moment as if thinking about what Nell had said. She was waiting for *his* response to see what he genuinely wanted. Paul raised his hand and caressed her cheek. Gently, his hand glided down towards her chin. Paul, then, tilted forward and kissed her lips tenderly. Shocked by his own actions and that Nell had allowed him to kiss her, Paul pulled away, examining how Nell would react. The fine line between friendship and lovers had been crossed, but was it something that Nell really wanted with *him*? Nell glanced at him, just as amazed. Paul waited to see if she would reject his advances, wanting to be assured. As brief was the kiss was between them, it seemed remarkably pleasant. Much to Paul's bewilderment, Nell tilted further and returned his kiss. It was innocent and genuine. Paul closed his eyes and opened his mouth slightly. He attempted to push his tongue in Nell's mouth, but felt her pulling away. Before she could do so, Paul pulled her closer to him. Once again, he opened his mouth and wrapped his tongue around hers, kissing her hungrily. Nell certainly was no experienced kisser as his girlfriends of the past, but Paul still liked kissing her. He had at last escaped the friend zone and was determined to move forward.

"Nell," he said, "If I were single, would you still want me, regardless of how others may feel about us? Would you be willing to date me even if you are colored and I'm white?"

"Yes."

Paul grinned and exhaled. As if, finally making up his mind, he gave her his reply.

"I still won't be single, since you are my new girlfriend. You are, aren't you?"

"As long as I am the *only* girlfriend, yes," said Nell.

"I'll have to talk to Nancy," Paul said. "She is not going to take the breakup well. I am just letting you know that. If we are going to be together, our relationship must be kept a secret. Do you agree?"

"Okay," Nell agreed.

"You also have to do as I say, no questions asked," Paul continued. "For one, I want you to start meeting me in the science lab in the mornings for now. I'll have everything arranged for us, but never mention us to your family or friends. Whenever we are in public, never do anything affectionate towards me nor argue with me. Don't expect me to treat you with respect or as a girlfriend out in the open."

Nell remained mute. As unkind as his words were, Paul knew that dating her would be a huge risk for them both. None of his family nor friends would ever approve of their dating each other and Paul had worked so hard to make progress with her. He didn't want to risk losing Nell in any type of way. Paul said nothing further to her as he got out of the car and walked away. He sprinted back into the building where Mrs. Simpson, the science teacher, was locking the science lab.

"Mrs. Simpson," Paul said, "Do you need help with prepping the science labs?"

"Hi, Paul," Mrs. Simpson said. "Thanks, but I have a 10th grader helping me prep for the science classes."

"Are you sure?" Paul said. "I would really appreciate it if I could help you. I need another recommendation for college, and this could be counted as a form of service since I am limited to what I can do. I work for my family and my only free time outside of sports would be in the mornings and you're usually here."

"Prepping usually doesn't take a long time..."

"Also, I needed to help tutor another student in science," Paul added. "I can do the tutoring after I finish prepping. I promise the classroom will be spotless and there will be no trouble whatsoever."

Mrs. Simpson rubbed her chin, thinking.

"Well," she said, "You are a good student and I've never had any issues with you before. Okay, but the lab better be prepped good and no tricks from that other student. I'll open the door to the 12th grade science lab in the mornings and you can go right in to prep and tutor."

"Thanks, Mrs. Simpson," Paul said waving goodbye to the teacher. He made his way to the gym where the cheerleaders were gathered for the end of the day. Nancy waved her farewell to her friends and ran up to Paul, giving him a brief kiss on the cheek. On the way to the car, Nancy discussed the new cheer routines and how excited she was about the upcoming game. Paul said nothing, knowing that the evening was going to be an unpleasant experience for them both.

After the difficult drive, Paul parked his car in front of the driveway to Nancy's home. Nancy was puzzled. Usually during that time, Paul would have made a quick stop to a fast food with her before he dropped her off home. Instead, he drove her straight home that day. Paul had been acting strange for the last few days, making her wonder why. He had been telling her that he was busy with school, but she began to have her own suspicions, especially when he was becoming noticeably less and less affectionate with her. He no longer held her nor kissed her the way that he had in the past.

"Thanks for taking me home," Nancy said, caressing the back of his neck with her hand. She waited for Paul to be affectionate towards her, as he had before, but he didn't. Instead, he tilted closer to the driver's door, furthering the distance between them.

"I can't see you anymore, Nancy," Paul said. He gazed out the window as Nancy began to sob heavily. Paul hated breakups. He knew that it would take a while for Nancy to come to terms with everything, but he had made a promise to Nell that he would only see her and be with her only. One aspect in his life that he could be honest with and still maintain control was his love life. He no longer wanted to date someone that he had no more romantic feelings for, even if that meant hurting Nancy and surprising the school.

"Why?" Nancy asked. "What did I do, Paul?" She began to cough between her cries. Her mascara ran down her cheeks, smearing her once flawless appearance.

"Nothing," Paul replied. "I just can't be with you anymore. I--." Paul stopped, catching himself in time. He didn't dare to tell Nancy that he was leaving her for another girl, especially for Nell. "I am too busy and need to keep my grades up, otherwise I won't be able to get into a good college." He knew that what he was saying was a great lie, but Nancy and the rest of the school would have bought it easily. Hence, not even suspecting anything more.

"But I love you, Paul," Nancy said. More makeup began to smear as the trails of tears covered her face. Her chest began to quiver heavily as she choked back a great cry. "I will do whatever it takes to still be with you. Just don't leave me." With despair within her, Nancy scooted nearer to him and draped her arms around him.

"Nancy, I'm sorry," Paul said, not returning her affections.

Distraught, Nancy got out of the car and rushed into her parents' home. She didn't even realize that she had left her belongings inside the vehicle with Paul. Paul sulked as he grabbed Nancy's books and other items. He knew that if he would have to return them to her the next day, he would have no choice but to address the breakup in front of their friends. Not wanting to do so, Paul left Nancy's possessions on the front porch. Paul could see that through a window of the home that Nancy was hysterically weeping to her mother as she made a futile attempt to comfort her.

Paul resumed his drive, halting by Henry's house. Mrs. Wilkerson waved at Paul, but he stopped the vehicle, parking it in the driveway. He climbed out of the car and approached her.

"Hi, Mrs. Wilkerson," he said.

"Hello, Paul," Mrs. Wilkerson said. "What brings you here today? Henry is out back helping his father."

"I'm not here to see Henry. I'm here to see you. You see, I need a favor."

Chapter 14

The next day, at the school, Paul arrived early. As promised, Mrs. Simpson had the door unlocked and Paul promptly placed the science books on the different desks and tables. On the wall, the teacher had notes written in her handwriting for Paul to write on the board. He hurriedly started to jot the notes down onto the board with the notes barely being legible. Paul hesitated, eyeing the sloppy handwriting and immediately erased it. Starting again, using clearer handwriting, he began to write the notes down again. With time barely on his side, he finally completed scribing the notes on the board. He placed the chalk back on the panel and hurried out of the school where students were starting to congregate. Paul spotted his friends near Steven's car. Hastily, Paul went up to Henry.

"Hey, I gotta go handle some business," Paul said. "I'll see you in homeroom."

"Okay, see you then," said Henry.

From the corner of his eye, Paul spotted Nell entering the building. His heart began to race with anticipation. Unfortunately, he also noticed Nancy in one of her friend's vehicle. Three girls were facing Nancy who was still immensely bawling over the breakup. She was waving her hands frantically and shaking within the vehicle. One of the girls sought to reach over to soothe the pained cheerleader, but Nancy just began to throw an even bigger fit by throwing herself around the passenger side of the vehicle, forcing the other girl to back away from her.

Standing between the school building and the car in the parking lot, Paul stood at the crossroads. He could still decide to move on with his new girlfriend or go back to his former girlfriend. He had been with Nancy since last school year and Paul knew that if he had changed his mind and wanted to go back to her, Nancy would forgive him and take him back. She had a deep fondness for Paul and would do anything to be with him. Paul still cared about Nancy, but to him, he did not see her as someone he wanted to be with any longer and saw her as just a friend. His relationship with Nancy was like many others he had. They spent time together sharing experiences to see how far the relationships would go and at some point, they ended.

Then, there was the quiet, unpopular girl, Nell. She was his complete opposite. Paul was loud and outgoing; Nell was quiet and cautious, but in a way, she completed him, and he saw himself wanting to explore something more with her. Sure, she was no outgoing cheerleader, but she had proven to him that beauty comes from within and that it was not about skin color. She was knowledgeable and held his hand, one that was different from hers and had been thoughtful in all her actions, touching his heart in a way it never had been touched before.

Entering the building, Paul made his way back to the science room. Inside he noticed Nell sitting in one of the desks, making his eyes light up. Remembering that first intimate kiss that they shared, he wanted to relive that moment, but saw an unanticipated tad of rage within Nell's eyes. Unsure of what was going on, yet still aiming to console her, Paul scooted into a desk next to hers and caressed her back with his hand.

"You look disappointed to see me," Paul said. "Is there something going on that you want to talk about?"

"I made a mistake," Nell told him. "I don't want to agree to any of the things you said."

Paul stared at her in disbelief. Needing a moment to process what he had just heard, he squinted his eyes, wondering if he heard her correctly. His mind began to race, unable to piece the words together that were flooding his mind to form a response. *She changed her mind!* With the words finally hitting him, Paul's heart sank, full of consternation. He slumped forward in the desk and struggled to clear his now itchy throat. For the first time in his life, he began to realize that he was about to cry over losing a girl. In an effort to restrain his now mounting emotions of sorrow, Paul reached into his pocket where he secretly hid the handkerchief Nell had given to him days before. He began to tighten and rub his fingers against it.

"Then, things are over before they start," Paul stated, still striving to soothe his nerves. "I dumped Nancy for you, and you are backing away from your promises this early."

Nell crossed her arms and threw him a no-nonsense glance before stating, "What kind of girl in her right mind would agree to anything you said yesterday? What kind of person do you take me for? 'No respect' from you? If you think I'm going to go back to being treated like garbage by you, you can date someone else. I thought you were turning into someone who was trying to better himself, but I guess I was wrong. You must really think lowly of me to make such a nasty request."

"One that wants to be safe in this town would agree," Paul fired back. "I didn't say any of that to make you feel less special. I want *you* to be safe because you *are* special to me. I already promised that I wouldn't mistreat you anymore and said I was sorry about everything that happened before. I *have* changed and I did it because I wanted to be with you! You already saw what happened when Nancy and Bill got mad because of what happened at the drive-in. Imagine how much worse it's going to be if they ever found out about us. If you think things are bad at this school, it'll only get worse if people like my grandfather ever found out. You don't know them like I do."

Paul grew subdued; his body posture began to soften with his spine curling slightly. His shoulders lowered. There was still a slight heaviness in his chest and a lump in his throat.

"If you still don't want to be with me, feel free to walk out the door," Paul said, his voice thickening. "If you still choose to stay, then stay with me. I care about you and would like for you to stay with me, but I will not force you into a relationship that you do not want to be in." He went to the teacher's desk and sat down on top of it. He nodded towards the door and waited for Nell to leave and walk out of his life as the person he desired. Heavily, Paul's eyes followed Nell as she went towards the door. Giving up, Paul couldn't bring himself to say more. He gave her a pained gaze before lowering his eyes. Once he looked up again, he found Nell standing at the door, facing him. She stepped towards him, causing Paul to burst into tears. He leapt from the desk and embraced her, crying tears of relief.

"Will you agree to my terms as my girlfriend?" Paul asked, wanting to be certain.

"Yes," Nell said, hesitantly. The bell rang for school to start.

"I want to see you again," Paul said. "Meet me here after school."

"But I have to take my sister back home."

"I'll wait. Drop her off and come back here. If the door is locked, just knock on it and I will let you in."

Nell nodded. Paul fastened his fingers with hers. Nell tried to pull away, but Paul's grip was still firm and locked. He drew her back towards him, kissing her, before letting her go to exit the classroom. Relieved, Paul wiped the remaining tears from his face and left the classroom. It did not take him long to realize that word had already spread about his breakup with Nancy. Students, especially the cheerleaders were whispering amongst each other and gawking at him. The last time something similar happened was before his relationship with Nancy and it didn't take long for other girls to try to offer themselves as replacements, like the opportunists they were.

"Hi, Paul," several girls flirted, some giggling.

Paul disregarded their flirtatious callings, hair tossing, and blinking eyes. A few guys were whispering and laughing once the news began to spread more than ever. Paul pushed through the crowded hallway and opened his locker, to find several folded pieces of paper in it. He unfolded a few to find out that they contained the names and numbers of several girls. Annoyed, he brushed the papers out of his locker and gathered his books for his next few classes. He spotted Martin in the hallway. No longer a target, Martin strolled by invisible to the eyes staring past him, vanishing. At least someone like him could find ways to disappear, which was something that Paul longed to do right now to escape the madness. Paul slammed his locker shut and entered the homeroom classroom and saw that Nancy was still agitated. She wore no makeup that day. Her nose and eyes were swollen and red. A tissue was pressed between her fingers. She coughed and sniffled back another cry. Paul sat down next to her, feeling responsible that he was the cause behind her tears. Apparently, several students within the class were oblivious to the situation and had a dubious look on their faces, including Bill. Paul took out a book and pretended to read it, hoping to avoid all the gossip. He felt a tap on his shoulder.

"Is it true?" Henry whispered. "Did you two really break up?"

Paul shut his eyes and dragged the book closer to his face. He refused to talk to anyone about the breakup. The time to end school couldn't come fast enough and it was just homeroom time!

"I'm so sorry, Nancy," a girl said to Nancy, who was also ignoring the other students.

Nancy blew her nose into her tissue and rested her head in the palm of her hand. The rest of the class had their eyes glued to the former couple, anticipating for possible accusations to be brought to the forefront.

"Who dumped who?" someone queried, loud enough for the class to hear.

"Paul dumped Nancy," somebody responded before promptly being shushed by another student.

Paul grimaced, keeping his eyes fixed on the pages in his book. He wondered how Bill would take things since he was overly protective of Nancy. Swiftly, Paul shot a glance at Bill, who was beaming as if he won a million dollars. When the bell rang to end homeroom, Bill was so ecstatic that he started swinging his arms while walking, whistling a cheerful tune. Paul rolled his eyes as he trailed his cousin to their next class. Fortunately, there was another math test scheduled and Paul never welcomed having a test so much in his life. Usually, Paul would have been one of the first few students to return their math test, but today was different. He kept his paper, working as slow as possible. Even Vernon Prichard, who was normally the last person to turn in his paper, turned his in before Paul. The class still was silent, waiting for him to finish. With forty minutes left of class, Paul turned in his paper, the final submission. Luckily, Mr. Thomas began teaching a new math formula, progressing the class. Occasionally, Paul would raise his hand, pretending that he didn't understand the new equations whenever he suspected that someone else was starting a conversation about him.

"Why can't we just work things out?" Nancy pleaded to Paul in the hallway, after class had ended. "We've been together for a while. I thought that things were going good between us. Just tell me, what's going on?"

"Not here, Nancy," Paul said, still walking.

"Then after school?"

"I can't. I'll be busy."

"Then I'll call you later tonight."

Paul quickened his pace, leaving her behind. He soon saw Henry standing by his locker with a wrapped plate. Paul sighed with relief. He had almost forgotten about yesterday when he stopped at the Wilkerson house and spoke to Mrs. Wilkerson. Paul had asked her if she could make her famous pound cake and give him several slices. Mrs. Wilkerson agreed, promising that Henry would give him the cake slices the next day at school. Henry handed him the plate and Paul put it into his locker.

"Wow," Paul said, "Tell your mother thanks for me. I owe her one."

"I don't think so," said Henry. "We owe you more than just a few slices of pound cake...So, what's with you and Nancy? Did you two really break up? There are lots of rumors spreading around the school about that. Four girls have already asked me to put in a good word about them to you; I asked them if I looked like a matchmaker to them."

"Yeah, we broke up. I don't want to talk about it."

"Wow, I never thought I'd see the day. Everyone thought you two were serious about each other. Did you at least get your ring back from her?"

"I never gave her my ring."

"Wow, I never knew that. I thought that since you two have been an item since last year, that you two would have been going steady by now. No wonder Bill has been prancing around all morning."

"I don't care about Bill." Paul closed his locker.

"I overheard Coach talking on the phone to some big shots over at South Louisiana University. He said that three universities are thinking about offering you a scholarship and he was still waiting to hear back. South Louisiana University is going to be watching the next game, so make sure you show up for practice tomorrow and don't get benched."

"I'll be there, he can count on me," Paul said.

"Good, the team needs you, buddy."

"Thanks," Paul said as both boys headed to their next class.

After school, Paul retrieved the plate of pound cake and entered the science lab. He placed the plate on the teacher's desk and began to erase the notes on the board. Mrs. Simpson entered the room with a 10th grade Negro student. Paul didn't know who the girl was, but apparently, she was helping the teacher and headed to the closet to retrieve the microscopes.

"I can do that," Paul told the girl, who faced the teacher.

"Paul, she is Geraldine," Mrs. Simpson said. "Geraldine is a 10th grader." She turned to the girl. "Geraldine, he is Paul, a 12th grader."

The girl smiled weakly.

"Mrs. Simpson," Paul said. "I still would like to help out more in the lab. In fact, I would like to do it more often. May I be in charge of the 12th grade lab and Geraldine can be in charge of the other labs. I just would like to come in every now and then to help whenever I am not doing things for the football team."

"That really is sweet of you, Paul," Mrs. Simpson said. "Well, since you are the senior, I guess I wouldn't have any problems with you assisting in the 12th grade lab. Here are the notes for tomorrow's class. Make sure it's on the board for tomorrow's class." She handed him two sheets of paper with writing and pictures for him to draw on the board.

"Yes, ma'am," said Paul.

Mrs. Simpson and Geraldine strolled out the classroom, leaving him alone.

Minutes later, Paul heard a knock at the door and opened it. He greeted Nell with a warm-hearted smile, letting her in. He locked the door and welcomed her with a deep kiss. She still seemed inexperienced but was getting better; Paul found her modesty to be cute and a little amusing.

"You came," Paul said, holding her close. He pressed his forehead against hers for a moment. He turned around and grabbed the plate of food off the teacher's desk. With his free hand, he held hers and guided her to two desks facing the window. There was an open field and a few buildings in the distance. A few clouds hovered in the sky, slowly making their way across to the other side of the building. "I'm glad to see you. Being here with you means a lot to me." He placed the covered plate on her desk. Nell uncovered it, revealing several pieces of pound cake. "I still feel bad about the ones you offered me a while ago. I hope that us eating some now could make it up to you."

Nell took a bite of a piece of pound cake, observing Paul as he did the same. He wrapped an arm around her, drawing her closer to him.

"Are you going to get back together with Nancy?" Nell asked. "I couldn't help but overhear your teammates saying that sometimes guys break up with their girlfriends to have something brief with another girl, and then go back to the original girl..."

"No," Paul responded, taking another mouthful of the cake. "I'd never do that to you. I already promised you that I wouldn't do anything to make you mistrust me. I'm keeping my word."

"Why not? She wants you back."

"Why are you bringing her up?" Paul asked, agitated. "This is *our* time together and I just want to focus on *us*. Yeah, she is a nice girl when she wants to be, but I want to be with *you*. That's why I left her."

"But why *me* though?"

"Because I like you more and you're more honest than she is," Paul said. "You aren't pretentious like everyone else I know. You don't smile in everyone's face and pretend to like them while trying to stab them in the back. I see enough of that from my own family with their dealings in the store and the community. You're also more beautiful than she is. Since I am being given a chance to be with you, I'm not trying to throw it all away to be with her or anyone else."

"But, what if your family ever finds out about us? Won't you get in trouble?"

"That's why I'm trying to get us to be extra careful around other people," said Paul. "My family is the worst in town for a reason and I don't even want to think about what they would do if they found out we are dating. My family and friends have eyes and ears everywhere. We are barely even safe here. I just wanted to spend time with you and be like a normal couple somewhere, even if it is in a classroom."

"I guess," said Nell. "Well, I have some good news. Thanks to you, I am doing better in the math class. I got a B on the last quiz and my homework scores are going up. I think I might actually pass the next test."

"That is good news. You're smarter than you think. Well, I have to go. I will see you tomorrow, Nell. In here once again, if you can make it in the morning. I'll be here waiting for you."

Paul leaned forward and kissed her. Like the soft pillows he had always imagined and desired, it all seemed innocent and welcoming. Getting passionate, Paul opened his mouth once more, finding her tongue. Swiftly and tensely, Nell broke the kiss. Paul grinned.

"You still seem nervous about kissing me," he said, snickering. "I take it that you aren't as experienced as I am.

Since we are together, let's be honest about a few things. Tell me, what's the furthest you've ever gone with a guy?"

Nell stood quietly, answering his question. Paul chuckled at the idea of being with a virgin. She was *too* innocent for the likes of him, but he still liked her. She had been willing to give him that chance and connection that he needed, so he would be willing to do the same for her.

"I see," said Paul. "Well, you already know about Nancy. I've had a total of four girlfriends, including you. I've only gone all the way with two."

"Did you and her...?"

"Yeah," said Paul. "Only because she wanted to. I didn't pressure her into doing it."

"I've never gone all the way... Are you expecting me..." Nell's voice trailed.

"No," said Paul, "I'm not expecting you to do anything, unless you want to. I might want a kiss every now and then, but since you're a virgin, I'm not going to push the issue. If that were important to either of us, that would have been brought up a long time ago. Well, Babe, it's time for me to get out of here. I will see you tomorrow. You don't mind if I start calling you 'Babe', right?" He gave a flirtatious wink, making Nell smile.

"Not at all," she said as Paul gave her a quick smooch before leaving.

Paul scurried to the gym where Nancy was waiting for him in the bleachers, alone. Paul rested next to her, keeping a distance between them.

"I didn't see you before school this morning," Nancy said, sniffling. "I was praying that you would somehow change your mind about me...about us...Still, I waited for you and will wait for as long as it takes to be with you again. Tell me, Paul, will there ever be chance that we will ever get back together?"

Paul's eyes met Nancy's. She was still hopeful and longed for him. A small part of Paul wanted to reach out and tell her how sorry he was that things had to end the way that they did, but he could not see himself lying to her nor himself any longer about the relationship they once had. He reflected on the time that he was still inside the same world that Nancy was a part of and asked himself, would things still have ended up the same. *Yes, he thought.* He hoped that one day, Nancy would find it in her heart to forgive him, but he needed to move on to the new chapter in his life, without her.

"No, Nancy," Paul said finally. "I'm sorry."

"I've been a good girlfriend to you, Paul..."

"You have and one day, you will make someone else the happiest person in the world."

"Why can't it be you?"

Paul frowned, leaving her question unanswered. Nancy scooted closer to him in the bleachers, closing the gap between them. She rested her head on his shoulder, tears from her eyes falling onto his letterman sweater. Paul wrapped an arm around her, providing her a tiny trace of comfort.

"I'll always love you, Paul," Nancy vowed. "I will never love anyone as much as I love you. I'll wait for you, no matter how long it takes."

"Nancy, don't wait for me," Paul stated before Nancy broke the embrace. She promptly ran off, her face still covered in tears.

Chapter 15

Paul finished stacking the last of the canned items. The evening had been slow at Sal's and there were still talks around town about how excited the community would be about the new Reynold's store that would be opening soon. In fact, Paul had seen how close the builders were to completing the project. The building was going to be bigger than Sal's and rumored to have already hired a number of unemployed individuals in the area. The Reynolds family also had a respectable reputation throughout the community. The owner, Samuel Reynolds was a middle-aged white man who had worked hard throughout the years, saving much of his money. Now everyone knew why, he wanted to open his own business and give others a chance to get ahead, through hard work as he did.

"Thank you, young man," an elderly woman said, pocketing her change in her tiny coin purse.

"Let me help you take your groceries to your car," Paul said, grabbing the bags. He helped the woman place the bags into her car and reentered the store. He was alone. His cousins and uncle were gone, stating that they had business to take care of. That was fine with Paul. He liked working by himself and not having to hear the constant sounds of their arguments and foul behaviors. Paul turned on the radio and began to listen to the music. He picked up a broom and began to sweep the floor. He whistled to the sound of the music in the background. When he finished sweeping, he began to straighten the items on the counter. Mrs. Wilkerson was still selling some of her homemade goods at the store, with permission from Abraham. Today, she had earned five dollars; Paul would have to give her the share of her profits and his grandfather, his five percent. Paul was surprised that Abraham allowed her to keep most of the money. His percentage was usually between twenty to thirty, but because of Paul, he agreed.

The clock ticked away, and his relatives were late. They stated that they would be back in an hour, but it had been three. Paul yawned and glanced out the window. To his surprise, he saw several police cars speeding down the street with their sirens blasting. In the distance, he spotted a bright light that flickered behind the buildings. Wondering what was going on, he turned the radio off and walked out of the shop to see several people outside of the other businesses talking and pointing. Paul approached Mr. Campbell, a barber who owned a shop next door.

"What's going on?" Paul asked.

"It's the Reynold's place," Mr. Campbell said. "It's on fire."

A firetruck zoomed past them and down the street. Paul rushed back into the store and dialed the number to hospital. He asked to be connected to his grandfather's room. Anxious, Paul began to bite down on a fingernail while waiting for his grandfather to pick up the phone. The phone continued to ring until finally, it was answered.

"Who is this?" Abraham demanded, his voice still weak.

"Grandfather, this is Paul," Paul said. "The Reynold's store, it's on fire."

There was a hush at the other end of the phone.

"Good," Abraham said. "Finally, those imbeciles can do something right."

"*You're* behind this?" Paul exclaimed. "I don't get it. For years, you've always told me to stick up for whites and how we all should stick together. The Reynolds are white and you're behind their store being burned to the ground!"

"They chose to build that store to interfere with my business," Abraham stated. "They had been informed to not build that store. I warn people once and if they don't want to listen, I will *make* them listen."

"So, *that* is why Bill, Wally, and Uncle Harry aren't at the store?"

"Partially, yes," Abraham stated with a dry laugh. "I had to send someone while you maintained Sal's. "

"Were you behind the burning of the Freedmen's School?"

"Oh no! I wouldn't burn *their* school down. Then those monkeys would have gone to Wood Oak High School years ago. They were all well contained in that filthy building they called a school on the other end of town. I'd be a fool to burn their school down intentionally."

"Grandfather, this had got to stop," Paul exclaimed. "You're practically on your death bed and you can't keep manipulating people to destroy everything. Can't you just use what time you have left to atone for your sins?"

"Paul," Abraham said, "I've worked hard to get to the top and I will see to it that nobody will take that from me, even in my old age. Everything I done, I've done for myself until now, I am leaving you my legacy and nobody, not even the Reynolds will rob me nor you of everything that I've worked hard to maintain. You question and blame me for using people? If you are at the top, you can get anyone to do anything that you want at your command. Do you want to control or be controlled? Your uncle and cousins are but mere lambs that can be slaughtered at any moment. Have you even considered *why* you were chosen to stay behind at Sal's, and they weren't? They are to take the fall should anything go wrong with my plans. They were there at the Reynold's business and you weren't. By now, you should have gone outside and have witnesses to say that you weren't there at the scene of the crime. It was all carefully thought out."

"The police could always go after you and turn you in. Not everyone in the department can be controlled by you."

"I'll be long gone before any of that ever happens," Abraham laughed. "Now, if there is nothing further, I'd like to rest. Goodnight!"

There was a click at the other end of the phone, ending the call. Paul stared at the floor, remorseful of the transgressions completed by his relatives. Time seemed to go by sluggishly with Paul sitting in the same slumped position. Then, minutes before closing time, Paul received a phone call from Wally requesting that he close the shop and that they would not be returning to the store that evening.

"Wally," Paul said, his voice depressed, "You know you don't have to do everything that Grandfather tells you to do."

There was a dull laugh at the other end of the phone. Disgusted, Paul hung up the phone and closed the shop. Powerlessly, he took another glimpse at the phone before getting into his car, knowing there was nothing more that he could do, with even the police under his grandfather's influence. He drove the long way home, avoiding the route that led to the Reynold's store. He avoided looking at the crowds of people who had gone out of their homes to point and talk about the fire. Finally making it home, Paul took out his keys, but noticed that the door to the home was unlocked, leaving a crack. On high alert, Paul put some keys between his fingers and balled his fist. Carefully and quietly, he widened the door and entered the home. He flicked on the lights and scanned the living room. Nobody was there. Paul scanned the kitchen and dining room; nothing. He looked in his grandfather's old office, nothing. Cautiously, Paul began to go up the stairs and go through each room. He noticed that someone had been in his room and that his closet and chest had been opened, but nothing was missing. Paul went through the other rooms, finally ending at his grandfather's room. On his grandfather's bed, The Album was opened and had a new entry: **Samuel Reynolds, 55, Shop owner, September 28, 1969.** Next to the entry were the letters: BD and DBB. Paul tried to scan his brain to remember what the letters stood for. He tugged at the hair on his scalp, recalling that BD meant, burned down. Not remembering what DBB meant, Paul paced about the room, unable to recollect. Finally, Paul grabbed ahold of The Album and flipped to prior entries, stopping on a page where there was a picture of a dead man lying face down and smiling men posing with their guns. DBB meant death by bullet.

Chapter 16

Days later, Paul held his school ring with thoughts of Nell. It was customary for guys to give their girlfriends their rings, especially if they were going steady with them. Since Nell had made him promise not to see any other girls, technically, they were steady. Deep down, he cared about Nell and couldn't see himself liking another girl as much as he liked her. Their relationship was still in the beginning stages, but Nell seemed special to him. He laughed, thinking of how she once spilled soda all over him and how much he got upset. Once he thought about the situation, he thought it was funny.

"As quiet as you are, you got fire," Paul said, contemplating about her. His grin widened remembering how shy Nell was during their first kiss together and how he had surprised her with a deeper kiss. "Whoever said girls like you are imperfect are damn wrong. You're the most perfect girl for me." He put on his shirt and covered it with his letterman sweater. He stuffed his ring inside of it and drove to school. "Well, Babe, if you're going to be my old lady, we might as well make it official."

On campus, Paul strolled past several students who were conversating about the sock-hop. He disregarded them, making his way to where he had wanted to be all morning. He locked the door behind himself and waited for Nell to show up. No matter how many times, they would meet up, Paul always sensed his heart skipping a beat for her. After hearing the knock at the door, he opened it and let Nell in. He locked the door once again and press his lips on hers. As expected, the kiss was beautiful, and his appetite never faltered for her.

"I missed you," he said, meaning every word. He drew her closer to him before leading her to the teacher's desk. He kissed her once more on the neck, pleased that he managed to make her slightly shiver from the passionate motion.

"I'm going to give you something," Paul said, sitting on the desk. Nell sat down next to him as he gave her his school ring. "I want you to have it. All guys give it to the girls that they are going steady with. Since we are going steady, I'm giving you mine. Unless, you are having second thoughts again, I want you to keep it." He smiled, no longer arrogant, but sincere.

He observed as Nell unhooked her necklace, placing the ring on it and hiding it, near her heart.

"There is a sock-hop today, as everyone knows," Paul continued. "Those are usually fun to go to. I wonder what songs they will be playing."

"But we can't go together," Nell said, resting her head on Paul's shoulder.

"We don't have to go to theirs," Paul said, wrapping an arm around her. "We can have our own. I want you to meet me back here after school, if you'd like to. I got a transistor radio that we can dance to. Sometimes, when the guys and I hang out in Henry's car, his radio doesn't work. That's when I got the radio, so we all could still listen to the music. That solved the music problem, but it didn't solve the disputes on which station we should all listen to."

"I'm not very good at dancing," Nell reminded him. "I'm not very good at anything."

"Don't sound like a square, Nell. You can just follow my lead," Paul said dropping down from the desk and taking her hand. "I owe you a dance, remember. It will be fun with just you and me anyway. By the time I finish teaching you, they will be requesting for you and me to dance on television!"

"You're silly, Paul," Nell laughed. Now off the desk, Nell followed Paul's lead as he began to dance with her, humming a tune from a song he had heard earlier that day from his car radio. Paul breathed in the alluring scent that radiated from Nell. It was a nice floral scent with a hint of vanilla. It smelled as beautiful as her calming spirit and Paul welcomed the peace that he was feeling, alone with her in that moment in time, until Nell inadvertently stepped on his shoes. It was a little humorous for Paul to be dancing with a girl who was not the picture-perfect dancer as Nancy had been, but Nell was still perfect in Paul's eyes. Paul shut his eyes for a moment from the pain and continued to dance with Nell. Nell tried to pull away, but Paul held her steadfastly, pulling her closer to him. "It's okay, Nell. Let's just keep going. You can do this."

Nell gradually picked up her head and stared at Paul's smiling face. He persisted to guide her in the dance until the bell sounded for school to begin. Paul bent forward and kissed her. Nell shyly returned the kiss. Abruptly, she let out a gasp as Paul lifted her off her feet in his embrace. He playfully spun her around in one short spin, making them both laugh uncontrollably.

"I will see you later, Babe," Paul said, lowering Nell back onto the floor. "I'll meet you back here later for our dancing date." He gave her a quick peck and hurried out the door. He walked with a bit of pep in his step, as the happiest guy at the school. Cracking a smile, Paul joined the homeroom class. He waited eagerly for his girlfriend to enter so that he could steal another glance of her. When she did, he could hardly pay attention in class, imagining spending more time with her. Remembering to lay low, Paul forced the smile off his face.

Paul was on top of the world until lunch time came around. He was sitting around his usual group of friends, sneaking glances at Nell until he saw Martin move towards her. Agitated, Paul zoned in on the other table across the cafeteria. He tried tuning out the conversations of his friends at the table and tried to see if he could make out the conversations that were going on at the other table, even trying to read their lips. Turning red, Paul knew that they were possibly talking about the sock hop and that angered him. Paul wanted to leave his table and bash his tray across Martin's head for having the audacity to speak to *his* girl. Nell was *his* girlfriend and he refused to share her with anyone. Paul averted his eyes and fought within himself to not go through with his plans to punch the living day lights out of Martin. Since his friends were leaving the cafeteria anyway, Paul followed them. He excused himself from the group and went into the boy's bathroom. He went inside one of the stalls and began to punch the walls of the stall with his fists, visualizing that they were Martin's face. Once he had finished having his fit of rage, he exited the stall to see that Henry was waiting outside the stalls, confused.

"What's going on?" Henry asked. "You were happy until we left the cafeteria. What happened?"

"That bastard," Paul grunted. "I just want to pound him."

"Who?"

"Don't worry about it," Paul said, heatedly moving past his best friend. He walked into the hallway and noticed Martin reading a book on the ground. Paul grabbed Martin by the shirt collar, lifting him up, and slamming him against the lockers. "Don't you ever talk to her again, you hear me!"

Martin's eyes widened as he stared back at Paul. His lips began to quiver. He raised his hands and lifted his arms in a surrender-like position, dropping his book. He gasped wildly as the collar from his shirt tightened in Paul's grip. Other students began to gather, speculating what all the commotion was about.

"Who are you talkin' about?" Martin asked, a tremor in his voice.

"You know who!" Paul said giving him another shove before letting him go. Paul stormed down the halls, leaving several students puzzled and whispering. He made his way to his next class, in a sour mood. He was outraged and once he was irate, it took him some time to calm down. Someone tried to take *his* Nell away from him, and it was a square like Martin! Martin could have any of the other girls at the school, except *his*. Paul dropped his pencil on purpose, and it rolled to the back of the classroom as planned. Paul retrieved his pencil, but not before shooting another incensed scowl at Martin, who flinched at the sight of the lethal stare. Paul noticed that Nell was deep into working on her assignment. He wanted to grab her and kiss her in front of Martin to show Martin that Nell was his, but that would have exposed both of them, frustrating him further. With his pencil in hand, Paul went back to his desk, still upset that he was envisioning the impossible. It didn't seem to be fair that everything he wanted to do with his girlfriend was not an option. He couldn't do anything with her in public, especially be affectionate. Paul was not used to having any type of limits set upon himself in his love life but being with Nell had changed everything. Everything was different and only because of something stupid as skin color. The whole thing was ridiculous the more he thought about it and he began to think about how absurd other people were to believe that something as small as that was a big deal and reason to not be with someone. Paul needed an outlet. He wanted to go with *his* girl to the sock-hop, the person that he knew would never be welcomed.

After school, Paul grabbed the transistor radio he had from his locker and made his way to the science room. He stared out the window, wishing that things didn't have to be difficult. He wondered if Nell felt the same way as she walked into the room. He intentionally did not lock the door; nobody ever came except for her anyway. He just wanted to be open in some way, even if it was something small as leaving the door unlocked.

"Paul?" Nell said, locking the door and stepping towards Paul. "Are you okay? You don't seem to be yourself. I heard that you almost got into a fight with Martin. How come? He usually keeps to himself."

"Are you having second thoughts about us?"

"What? No, why?"

"I saw you talking to that other guy," Paul said, bitter at thoughts of himself being replaced. "He wanted to take you to the dance, didn't he? Something that I could never do." His voice began to crack. "I-it's not right. You're *my* girlfriend, not his!"

"We can always still go."

"No, Nell," Paul said. "We could never go. I couldn't offer you a dance in the cafeteria, no matter how much I want to. All we got is this damn room. I just feel ashamed that I can't take you. I know how badly you want to join the others, but all we got is this radio."

"With music that I can't dance to," Nell reminded him. "I have two left feet, remember."

Paul laughed, looking less despondent. He took out the transistor radio and turned on some music. They both took their shoes off and began to dance slowly. Nell smiled with her arms wrapped around Paul's shoulders and his around her waist. She didn't step on his toes as much. While the music was slower than they both were used to, it seemed more peaceful to them. Paul paused their slow dance and stared into Nell's brown eyes and she gazed into his grey eyes. His lips soon touched her lips. Nell seemed more comfortable kissing him without that strange doubtful feeling. There was a time when she used to look into his eyes and hated him, but now those fears were replaced with yearnings and affection. Unsurprisingly, his were the same. Soon, the radio began to play a faster song and Paul smirked. He began to show her how to do moves like "The Hitch Hiker" and "The Hully Gully" as the radio blasted with the different songs.

"You're going too fast," Nell laughed, trying to follow his moves.

"I thought all colored people could dance," Paul joked.

"Maybe all except me," Nell said, rolling her eyes.

"It's fun," Paul said, laughing. "Don't you ever watch American Bandstand? You can listen to all the music and see all the dancing on that show. That's what I do."

"I've never been good at dancing. You already know that! I don't have a television at home, so I can't watch that show."

"That's ok; I was the dancing king at all the dances," Paul joked. "Just watch me and do as I do."

Nell watched Paul and tried to mimic his moves, sometimes failing miserably. They both laughed as the music continued to play. Grabbing his sides, Paul laughed hysterically when Nell attempted to do "the Watusi" dance.

"Go to the sound of the music and bend your arms more," Paul said, "You're looking like a wild windmill with your arms all over the place."

"You should have said something before I did it!" Nell giggled.

"Don't worry," he said. "We are going to get all these dances perfected and then one day, I'll be able to flip you over my back and everything."

"That will *never* happen, Paul," Nell exclaimed, beaming with her eyes wide.

"I got you to stop stepping over my feet, didn't I?" Paul replied, grinning. "Even if we have to practice every other day, you will be good at dancing one day." He pulled her closer to him, giving her another smooch. "Well, Babe, I have to bail. I'd say we had fun today. What do you think?"

"Yes, we did," Nell said, returning the kiss. "And Paul, do me a favor."

"What's that?"

"Apologize to Martin. He is harmless and there is no reason for you to be jealous of him. He is a really nice guy once you get to know him. Do it for me."

Paul exhaled and bent forwards slightly. He let out a low grumble but nodded in agreement.

"Okay," he agreed. "I promise, I will. I'll see you tomorrow." Paul grabbed his radio, turned it off, and walked out the door. He closed the door behind him. He quickened his pace and hurried to change out of his school clothes into his practice clothes. He met up with the other football players who had gathered in the gym for practice that day. The weather was looking terrible, and the coach had changed the practice site to the gym for conditioning. Paul had made it just in time without a minute to spare. Practice was short that evening and ended at the same time as the sock-hop event. Once practice was over, Paul changed back into his regular clothes and waited outside of the cafeteria for his cousin, Bill. Minutes later, Bill walked out of the cafeteria where the sock-hop was taking place. Bill asked Paul if he had any objections to him asking Nancy out. Paul informed him that he didn't mind if he asked out his ex. He had gotten over Nancy and was happy to be with Nell. Paul had other plans and things to worry about. One of them included finding a place to go on a real date with his girl. He had grown tired of sneaking around the school, and he was sure that she was probably just as tired. Knowing that there would be no safe place within the parish, he would have to find a different place to spend time with her.

After work, Paul drove to The Movie Pit drive-in where he had the soda encounter with Nell. He still felt remorseful for her losing her job because he was a jerk that night. Paul walked inside the crowded concession and saw the manager named Douglas. He asked if there were any other drive-ins in any of the other nearby parishes. Douglas told him that there was an old one, but it only showed older movies and would be a drive out of the way. That sounded perfect to Paul. He memorized the name of the street and decided that would be the perfect place to be with Nell.

Chapter 17

Throughout the day, Paul waited for the most opportune time to apologize to Martin, but so far, he had been out of luck. Martin was good at hiding when he was out of the classroom. The only time Paul would ever see him outside of the classroom would be when they both were in the cafeteria. Ever since Paul had confronted Martin, the teen who once was finally starting to sit down in the cafeteria was once again hiding. Whenever Martin would have to eat, he'd quickly devour his food, hardly chewing and swiftly made his escape into one of his spots around the school.

The cafeteria was serving meatloaf that day, much to Paul's disappointment. He wanted to take his time and enjoy his meal, but he was on a mission and luckily, he made it to the cafeteria before Martin did. Paul gulped down his food and spotted the teen in line waiting for the cafeteria worker to fill his tray. Now, in the room, Martin stood by the door near the garbage cans. Hastily, he partially ate his food and dumped the rest.

Paul promptly rose from his table and began to make his way towards the garbage cans. Martin flinched at the sight of Paul. He shoved his tray into the counter and rushed out of the cafeteria. Paul swore under his breath and tossed his tray onto the counter, not dumping its contents into the trash. Martin sped down the hallway, running as fast as his legs could carry him, becoming almost a blur. Paul chased after him. Martin rushed past the boy's restroom and the trophy case. His shoes made a loud squeak as he made a turn heading towards the auditorium. Breathing heavily, Paul persisted to chase after him. Soon, Martin shoved the auditorium doors open, running down the aisle. Inches behind him, Paul reached to grab him, but Martin made a sharp turn, entering the doorway to the stairs that led to the stage. Both teens ran onto the stage with Martin's breathing now becoming labored. He ran to the other set of stairs, catching himself before he stumbled. One of Martin's shoes flew off, hitting Paul. Paul fell and crash into Martin. In desperation to defend himself, Martin began to deliver blows with his fists at Paul, who pushed himself off the other teen.

"Stop, I want to talk," Paul shouted.

Martin attempted to raise himself off the floor but stumbled back down. The pencils and pens in his pocket fell, scattering throughout the ground. With his arm, Paul tackled Martin to the wall, pinning him.

"Get off me," Martin hollered, unable to move.

"Listen to me," Paul yelled. "I'm trying to apologize."

Both teens struggled to catch their breath. Immediately, Paul backed away, gasping for air. He fell back to the ground, catching himself with his hands. Martin slid to the ground, just as out of breath as his chaser.

"I-I'm sorry," Paul said. His chest rose up and down with his labored breathing. Grasping ahold of a nearby pen, Paul rolled it over towards Martin.

Martin snatched the pen. Still heavily breathing, he grabbed ahold of the other pens and pencils. He stuffed them back into his front pocket. He scooted to the side of the entrance and picked up his shoe. He put it back on his foot. Gradually, he rose to his feet, keeping a close eye on Paul. With a watchful, yet contemptuous glance, Martin hobbled away from Paul back to the doors of the auditorium. Paul remained on the ground. He heard the bell chime, making him toss his head back repeatedly against the wall. Paul sluggishly rose to his feet. His leg stung him. Paul moaned from the pain, gripping his leg. Gritting his teeth, he limped back towards the entrance of the auditorium. Leaving Paul behind, Martin exited the room. Paul could hear students talking and walking about on the other side of the door. He had kept his promise.

Chapter 18

For the next few days Paul thought about his family. Sure, they tolerated each other at the store, but Paul wanted for all the bitterness to end between them. He wanted to have faith that maybe there would be a possibility that things would get better before Abraham's passing and that they would be a true family once again. Out of the three, Paul chose to speak first with the cousin that sat near him, Wally.

"I don't want any more animosity between us," Paul said to Wally. "I know that you don't believe me when I say that I have no plans on keeping things for myself, once Grandfather dies. I know that you and the rest of the family have been struggling and I want to make things right. You all can have the cabin, the other houses, and the store. I don't know exactly how much he plans on leaving me as far as money is concerned, but I will make sure that it is split evenly towards everyone."

Wally yawned as he stretched. He shook out his arms and rolled his shoulders. Both he and Paul were sitting behind the counter while Bill was sitting in a chair to the side, reading a car magazine. The day had been pleasant, mainly because Harry was not there. He was at the hospital visiting Abraham. The store was empty of customers and had a mere fraction of supporters since the day the Reynold's store burned and its owner "missing."

"That's very generous of you, Paul," Wally said, beaming. "To think of us. You've always been considerate of others and we all appreciate your generosity."

Bill snorted, flipping the page of the magazine.

The door to the shop opened and all three young men turned to the door. It was a middle-aged Negro man that none of them had ever seen before. He wore a faded solid grey shirt with solid brown jacket and solid black slacks.

"Yeah?" Wally asked.

"Sir, I am from out of town," the Negro man said. "I am looking for North 7th Street."

"Keep driving past five lights and make a right turn," Wally said. "You should run right into it."

"Thank you," the Negro man said, leaving the store.

Bill curled his lip and waddled out of his chair. He yanked some tissue from his pocket and began rubbing the back and front door handles with it. He hurled the tissue into the trashcan. With that, he spun on his feet and sat back down near the register.

"Dumbass should have gone through the back," Bill muttered. "He's old enough to know that, fuckin' idiot."

"It's 1969," Wally sighed. "Everyone comes through the front, including the colored people. They've been doing that for a while. Today should be no different."

"Our shop, our rules," Bill replied.

"It's not *your* shop," Wally laughed, opening a newspaper. "Hmmm... artificial sweeteners with cyclamates have been banned...good thing we never carried that in the store... Paul, what does Mrs. Wilkerson use in her baked goods?"

"I dunno," said Paul. "I've always been told that she uses plain old sugar."

"Did you give her the money she earned from her sales this week and put aside Grandfather's cut?" Wally asked.

"Yeah, but I gave it to Henry," Paul said. "He said he would give it to her when he left the store yesterday."

"Did you get his signature?"

"No."

"Next time don't give him anything unless he signs the tab," Wally instructed. "He could easily just take the money and his mother could come in later and say we didn't pay her. Friend or no friend. Write down the date, amount of money given, items that were sold and how many, and have him sign his name. When you see him at school tomorrow, tell him to come back to the store to give us his signature."

"That flake probably wasted it all on smokes if he did keep the money," Bill grunted.

"I'll talk to Henry the next time I see him," said Paul. "My mind must have been preoccupied. I'll remember next time."

"We all make mistakes," Wally said looking at his watch. They still had three hours until closing time. All duties had been performed. Inventory had been checked and modified, the shelves have been restocked, the floors had been swept, etc. There was nothing more to do. Things were getting tedious.

Bill's eyes began to close, causing him to lean forward. A loud snore escaped his lips, waking him back up. Bill's head jolted up, but his eyes soon began to close again, repeating the drowsiness. Eventually, Bill fell completely asleep.

"I'm sorry about the fallout between you and Grandfather," Paul said to Wally. "I know you had your reasons for doing what you did, but I had nothing to do with Grandfather's decisions about his punishments."

"What's done is done," Wally said. "I have had lots of time to think about that day and I do not blame him for not wanting more to do with me. I am pleased that I was at least able to apologize for taking his money. I just wanted to get a safe place set up for mom, Bill, Linda, and myself. Right now, I have been able to save some money and I should be able to find a nice place soon, but I don't think Pop will be willing to allow mom to leave with us. You know, mom was always close to your mother, Aunt Helen. The two were best friends, even. I remember how mom and Aunt Helen used to talk daily and when I was six, I used to brag about wanting to marry her one day. She was so kind and beautiful." He smiled, having a long gaze as if reminiscing about pleasant years past.

"But if you were Grandfather's protégé, why were you living with Uncle Harry?"

"Pop and my father were extremely close," Wally explained. "When my real father passed, Pop begged Grandfather to adopt me. I guess you could say that he still wanted a living piece of his brother, I don't know; I was a toddler when my real parents died, and I can only go by what Grandfather told me."

"Do you think it's true about what he said about your real father and my mom?"

"I would not know the entire truth behind that," Wally said. "But, it must have been horrible for Grandfather to place my father in The Album. I was surprised that Grandfather wanted to have anything to do with me, considering how my parents grew out of his favor, but he said that I had potential and began mentoring us both. At least, until I lost his favor as well."

"Like that saying goes, people make mistakes," Paul said. "You learned from them and like other people, you deserve a second chance. Remember when you, Grandfather, and I used to have nice dinners back at the house? I'd like for us to do that again, even if it is without Grandfather. Heck, we can even invite Linda when she comes back home from college, Aunt Henrietta, and even cranky Bill. I'm not sure about Uncle Harry, but he's gonna have to change his ways if he wants to be included with us."

"You almost sound like a hippie," Wally laughed. "If you want to have any dinners with everyone, Pop would only allow it at his house."

"I don't care," Paul responded. "I just want for us to all go back to being a real family for a change. It's ironic to be part of The Family when our own is in shambles."

"You're right," Wally agreed. "That would be nice, and I'd like nothing better."

Chapter 19

Paul whistled cheerfully. The football team managed to win their district but lost the regional. Coach Anderson had informed Paul that four universities were interested in offering him scholarships to play football. He was excited. Two were in Louisiana: The University of South Louisiana and The University of Baton Rouge. Two were out of state: The Semmes College in Michigan and Gulf Shores University in Alabama. All four schools were offering Paul full scholarships and were reputable. Unable to decide which school to go to, Paul wanted to talk to Nell first to see what her plans were. More than anything, he wanted her to have a future with him. But the question that haunted him in a way was, would Nell still want a future with him beyond the high school. They had been through a lot together and still he had not told her those three words that he had never uttered to any girl before. In his heart, he knew that of all the girls that he had been with, those three words were meant for him to say to Nell. Tonight, would be a good time to have his questions answered and thoughtful words spoken.

Earlier that day, Paul had informed Nell that they would be going on their real first date outside of the school and that it would have to be in secret and at night. Normally, Paul would have knocked on the front door and introduce himself to the family before taking a girl out, but that was out of the question for them both. The only other option was to sneak out and meet. Nell had given Paul her address and he found the small yellow shotgun house a few blocks away from the school. It was much smaller than the houses that Paul was accustomed to, even the Wilkerson family had a larger house. None the less, that meant nothing to Paul, the person he cared about lived there. He parked on the dark street and waited. Luckily, majority of Nell's neighbors were inside their own homes attending to their needs. The only people that were outside were busy in their own conversations or sleeping outside in old chairs on their porches. Paul waited silently, hoping that time would pass by without incident. A walking Negro couple passed his car, giving bewildered looks, but said nothing, resuming their stroll down the neighborhood street. The lights were still on at Nell's parents' home and the window that she said she would meet him at was still lit. Once the light went out, Paul spotted movement near the window. It lifted and he saw his girlfriend climbing out. She carefully dropped down onto the ground and closed the window behind her, leaving a barely noticeable crack. It was 8 p.m. and on time. Nell crossed the street, nearing Paul's car. Paul motioned for her to climb into the back. Nell opened the door and climbed inside. She closed the door and Paul began the drive.

"Babe, remember to stay down," Paul reminded her. He drove to the outskirts of the Negro area and was soon back into the familiar downtown area that was brightly lit. Paul soon drove down the street seeing more and more familiar buildings and people, who waved to him. He turned on the radio, hoping to add a little bit of entertainment for Nell as she hid in the back and to help keep himself calm. "Nell, what did you think about the test Mr. Thomas gave out today?"

"It was hard, but I think I passed," Nell said. "Thanks to you for helping me study. How do you manage to stay smart, be good at sports, work, and have time to see me?"

"It's called balance," Paul said. "Remember out of everything, you're the most important to me."

"How come?"

"Because you're my old lady and always will be," Paul chortled.

"I *must* be an old lady for you to be driving me around like a chauffeur."

"It beats being stuck in that boring classroom. I'm sure you've gotten tired of just hanging around there as much as I am. How'd the rest of your day go after school?"

"It went fine," said Nell. "What do you think about what occurred to the Reynold's store? Isn't it a shame! I never talked to Mr. Reynolds personally, but I heard that he was a nice man who was nice to everyone and he planned to hire some Negroes. I was going to see if I could possibly work there myself, but then, boom, more evil stuff transpired. Nobody knows what happened to him. They say he went missing, but don't you think it's strange how his store burned to the ground and then he just disappeared? That's Wood Oak for you!"

Beads of sweat began to form on Paul's forehead. He wiped it away with his hand, unsure of what to say.

"Yeah, that's Wood Oak," Paul said, after clearing his throat. "So, um, Babe, is your family having another dinner together this Sunday?"

"Yeah," said Nell, "I just wish that you would be a part of it. It's a time where were all get together, eat, joke around, and in the case of my sister, Claudine, getting into everyone's business but her own."

Paul laughed.

"It does sound fun, and I wish I could hear the conversations that go on around the table," he said. "My family used to have them years ago, before my parents died in the car accident. Afterwards, it was just my grandfather, Wally, and me for a while. Then just my grandfather and me. Soon, it will just be me, alone. I tried reaching out to my relatives and they seem to be wanting to reconnect. I intend to before the year is up. I don't want everyone to keep having this rift over money because at the end of the day, money cannot offer you things that people can. Money cannot offer you companionship nor love. It just sits there, causing everyone to hate each other and encouraging fake loyalty."

"People can be the same way, you know."

"Yeah, but at least with people, you have a greater chance of finding a few who are genuine and sincerely care about you."

"Sounds like you are lonely where you live. I hope you do reconnect with your family."

"Thanks, I hope so...So, Babe... At your old school, tell me about the best teacher you had and the worst teacher you had."

"Hmmm," said Nell. "I remember having Mr. Harris. He was smart, wise, and a good teacher. He taught economics. I remember him telling me that before you leave a bank or a store, to always count your money twice in front of the teller or clerk. Let me see...My worst teacher was Mrs. Petri. She used to be my old English teacher. One day we did an assessment, and she told the class that a few people did well on it and named me amongst the top in the class. But then, she added that she didn't know how I managed to be one of them. When my mother found out, she went straight to the principal's office and had a meeting with both the principal and Mrs. Petri. Mrs. Petri stated that I would never get any higher than a C in her class. Then my mother said that they would see her back over there in that office!"

"Really?" exclaimed Paul. "I hate that. That reminds me of Mrs. Nelson. I had her for English in middle school. We all had to write an essay on what we thought the future would be like and I wrote about having solid gold cars and she said it was absurd and failed me on the assignment. I did well on my other assignments, so I still passed the class. Let's see...My best teacher was my former Spanish teacher, Ms. Edwards. She was fresh out of college and everyone liked her."

"Why?"

"Because she was good looking," Paul laughed. "I don't remember learning a thing! How did the other students act at your school?"

"Most students got along and worked hard. Many of us took our education seriously but we had a few students who would be teased about 'actin' white' or being 'uppity Negroes.' It was almost more accepted by a few students to talk with poor grammar, but they knew better because they took English classes. Sometimes there were differences in socioeconomic classes. Nobody wanted to be on welfare, but students didn't know they were poor until someone would tell them. They always thought they were doing okay because they had enough to eat. If you had more relatives at the school, it would be better for you, especially if they were more influential."

"Were the guys treated better than the girls?"

"It depends; the guys were mainly pushed into doing more sports related activities like football and basketball. When it came to academics, the boys didn't take many advanced classes in math and science unless it was pushed by their parents or if the boy was super smart. For the girls, it was mainly courses focused on the home like home economics. They didn't think the girls would do well in science and math."

"Did you have any good moments at the school?" Paul asked.

"There were good moments," Nell said. "We had assemblies and had some Negro motivational speakers who would talk to us about the importance of having an education. Some people would talk about sports and music. Once a month, we would have a dress up day and students would go to school in their church clothes. Whenever a Negro man or woman would be on television, that would be the talk of the school, at least for the ones who had televisions. We also had our own sporting activities, like Wood Oak does...How far are we going out? We've been traveling for a while."

"It's just a little further. You trust me, don't you?"

"I'd trust you a little more if I knew *where* we were going."

"You'll see," Paul said, turning into the old drive-in that Douglas had told him about. It certainly wasn't like the one in

Wood Oak. The one in Semmesville was older and had five cars in the lot, mostly older cars and older couples. Paul parked his car far away from the rest and walked off. He entered the building and purchased some popcorn and sodas. He went back to the vehicle and sat next to Nell in the back. He handed her a drink and placed the popcorn between them. "We had to drive a little further to the next parish. Nobody really goes to this drive-in because they show the older movies, but it beats that classroom, and we can be here together."

Nell smiled as Paul wrapped his arm around her shoulder and began to eat some of the popcorn. Paul kissed Nell's forehead and playfully fed her some popcorn every now and then. Nell mischievously smirked at the drink in her hand.

"Are you sure you want to give *me* drinks at a drive-in?" Nell joked.

"Don't you dare!" Paul laughed, cuddling her. Paul gave her a gentle squeeze. Everything was perfect and Paul knew what to do to end the night in the best way possible, knowing he had never done it before with any of the girls from his past. After the movie ended, Paul got out of the car and discarded the trash. He got back into the driver's seat and drove a short distance further into the swamps. Soon, he stopped the car and parked it.

"What's wrong?" Nell asked, evaluating Paul's actions.

Paul got out of the car and opened the door to the backseat. Suspicious, Nell scooted further away from him. Her lips began to tremble with skepticism in her eyes. Paul extended his arm and held his hand out towards her. Nell's eyes widened at the gesture.

"Come on out," Paul insisted, calmly.

Taking a deep breath, Nell reached out to Paul's hand. Interlocking them, Paul helped Nell out of the vehicle. They were alone, with the moon and stars lighting the darkness around them. Wrapping his arms around his love, Paul uttered the words to Nell that he meant with all his heart.

"We are now out in the open," he said. "I wanted to tell you that I love you, Nell."

Before then, he had never uttered those words to any girl. She had been the first and he meant every word, anticipating that one day she would feel and say the same to him. He had never fallen so hard for a girl, especially one as calm as Nell. Being his total opposite, it was as if she completed him. Paul loved their differences and enjoyed seeing her slowly opening up to him, even to the point of agreeing to sneak out with him, making her more rebellious than before. Paul's heart swelled when Nell wrapped her arms around him.

"I love you too, Paul," she said, her lips meeting his.

Knowing that it was months before their high school graduation, Paul wanted to see what Nell's plans were for the future. He knew that it wouldn't be fair to be with her and disappear out of her life upon graduation. He had to tell her that he would be leaving, eager for a chance that she would possibly go with him.

"We only have a few more months left of high school," Paul said. "Afterwards, I would like for you to leave with me, if you are willing. I want us to have a life together outside of Wood Oak."

"But what about our families?" Nell asked.

"I'm fine with leaving mine behind. Especially, if they wouldn't want us to be together. You are free to do whatever you choose with your family. I just wish for you to stay in my life."

"I still want to be in contact with my family. I love them and they wouldn't mind our relationship, if we give them time to get over it."

"You are lucky to have a forgiving family, but it is best if nobody ever knew. If they ever found out, they must never mention us or our relationship."

"Paul," Nell said. "I know we live in a prejudiced town, but I think you are still holding back things from me. I want you to be more open and honest. Why are you more fearful of your family than all the other prejudiced ones around town?"

Paul briefly held his breath before exhaling. Beads of sweat began to form on his brow. He licked his lips before clearing his throat.

"If my family ever found out about us, there would be no place to run or hide," he said. "They hate people who are not like them with a passion, and they have done a lot of horrific things that even the worst stories on television wouldn't even show. I never want them to harm you or your family. Trust me when I say that I don't want anything bad to happen to you or them."

He gazed into his love's eyes. She seemed to be understanding and asked no more questions about it. Paul was relieved. It was nearing 11 p.m. and Paul wanted to make sure that Nell was home and safe.

"It's getting late," said Paul, wrapping his arm around Nell. "I better take you home." He kissed her forehead before opening the door to the backseat. Nell climbed in and watched as he went to the front of the car. They drove silently for several miles until there was the boisterous sound of a car horn trailing them from behind. Paul signaled for Nell to lower herself further in the backseat. The other car pulled to the side of Paul's. It was Henry's vehicle and inside was his friend and two other guys from the football team. They had been out partying; something that he too used to do.

"Hey, Paul," Henry called out, "you feel like drag racing tonight?" The other guys cheered in agreement. Henry revved up the car, smirking at the red light and back at Paul.

"Nah," Paul yelled over. "It's late. I have to get home."

"You're no fun anymore," another member of the football team shouted out as Henry sped away into the night.

Paul paused and began to drive again.

"Nell," he said, "in a few minutes, we should be back at your house. I need you to quickly go back through your window so that I know you are safe. I can't stay long."

"Okay," said Nell.

A few minutes later, the car stopped in the same dark street where Paul had met her earlier. Feeling the warmth of Nell's hand reaching from the back of the seat, Paul turned his face to see Nell, bent over the front seat. She reached forward and kissed him quickly, sending shockwaves through Paul's heart.

"I love you," Nell said, quickly exiting the car.

"I love you too, Babe," Paul said, watching her cross the street back to her window. She raised the window and climbed through it, back into the house. She smiled and closed the window behind her. Grinning, Paul took off to return to his own home.

Chapter 20

A tiny ray of light shined from the lampposts between the outside world and the inner world of the Boudreaux house that had been under the power of Harry Boudreaux. His daughter, Linda, was doing one of her rare and brief visits that day away from her nursing school studies. She was now in the nursing program and was doing exceptionally well. Like her mother, Henrietta, she ate noiselessly and took tiny bites of the pot roast that had be prepared for them to consume that night.

Paul was also at the table. He had not eaten dinner within their household since he was thirteen years old, days before Abraham had disinherited everyone, except him. Unlike the wide atmosphere of Abraham's dining room, the dining room in Harry's home was exceptionally small and the air was full of distrust and bitterness. Next to Paul was an empty chair that used to be occupied by his grandfather.

There was absolute silence except for the hungry noises made by Bill who quickly gobbled down his food. Barely taking a bite, he swallowed most of his food. Everyone at the table knew that was due to his suppressed anxiety when around Harry. No longer the bully with the tough exterior, Bill sunk lower at the table next to his father, Harry, who sat tall, taking the dominant stance. Harry's eyes grew colder the longer he observed his son. His eyebrows lowered and pinched together at the sight of Bill reaching for another dinner roll. Suddenly, Harry slammed down his fist against the table, surprising everyone.

Wham!

Everyone at the table jumped at the sound and Bill quickly yanked his hand back towards himself and under the table. Harry refocused his eyes upon Paul. Jittery, Paul rubbed the back of his neck when his uncle spoke.

"I heard you got offered four scholarships to play football," Harry said.

"Yes," said Paul, after clearing his throat. "I'm still trying to decide on which offer to take."

"You must really like making decisions," Harry said, a hard edge to his voice. "Decisions about school, decisions about money, and decisions into tricking my father into leaving you everything we all worked hard for."

"I didn't make any decisions on what Grandfather did with his will," Paul said. "Anything he did with regards to that is all on his own."

"Then you come back into my home," Harry continued, "eating what little scraps of food we have. What are your 'decisions' about the rest of us once my father is dead and gone? You going to throw us all out onto the streets, penniless?"

Paul's eyebrows raised and his head drew back quickly. This was not how he planned for the evening to go. His plans for a reconnection seemed even more distant than ever. It was surprising to Paul how Harry had managed to keep a tight tongue about his feelings all those previous years.

"With all due respect, Pop," Wally said. "It was Paul who paid for the groceries and he has expressed many times that he is willing to share the assets equally. He has no plans on taking our home, the cabin, nor the store."

"And you believe him?" Harry said. "You all forget that I, too, was raised by my father and I know how he operates. I wouldn't expect anything less from Paul."

"Maybe this was a bad idea," Paul muttered, wiping his mouth with his napkin. "I'm going to be heading back home." He turned to his cousins and aunt. "It was nice seeing you again, Linda and Aunt Henrietta. I'll see you at school, Bill. Wally, I'll see you back at the store."

Paul frowned before making his exit. He entered the darkness of the night seeing only the rays of light from the streetlamps as small signs of comfort. The icy cold surrounded him, stinging his skin. He blew into the palms of his hand and walked across the street, back again into the lonely home. He forced back the tears that began to brim his eyes. Sniffling heavily, he entered the kitchen and opened the cabinet that contained two bottles of his grandfather's favorite liquor. Paul yanked one of the bottles out at the neck and held it close. He sunk to the floor, opening the top which he hurled across the floor. Repeatedly, he hit the back of his head against the wall. Bringing the bottle of booze to his lips, Paul opened his mouth, swallowing as much of it as he could in one gulp. Bits of the liquid exploded from his mouth as Paul coughed from the stinging liquor going down his throat. Forcing another swig of drink, Paul continued to swallow its contents in vain attempts to ease his ever-growing pain.

Chapter 21

"I asked Nancy out and she finally said yes," Bill said, proudly.

It was another monotonous day at Sal's. Despite their grievances from the night before, Paul and Harry made no mentions of what had occurred during dinner and did their regular duties with Paul stocking shelves, taking inventory, and making the store presentable alongside Bill while Harry managed the store with Wally assisting him throughout the day. With a gruff, Harry went to the back of the store into the small office, leaving the three cousins alone.

"I thought Paul was dating her," Wally said.

"No," replied Bill, "they broke up weeks ago."

Wally's eyes fell upon Paul, who was indifferent as he replenished the shelves. Paul did not care that Nancy was now dating Bill. He had already moved on and was happy with his own relationship. He was even glad for Bill, who was now grinning from ear to ear. He didn't seem to be as grouchy as he usually was. Instead of slamming and shoving things, he was working serenely as never before. He even began whistling, shocking everyone.

"And, you are okay with this, Paul?" Wally asked.

"It's fine," said Paul. "We already talked about this weeks ago." He put the last canned item on the shelf and moved behind the counter where his cousins were. All three listened as the radio began to talk about the news regarding local protests at several universities about hiring Negro faculty and offering Negro programs. Bill turned red in the face.

"They don't need no fucking programs," he declared. "They need to just be shot and killed. All of them!"

"Hey," said Wally, "times are changing, and things are being catered more to them."

"You can't even turn on the radio without hearing about their shit," Bill stated furiously. "Day and night, that's all that they talk about. Then they had that damn Loving couple fuck things up. Makes me sick to my stomach thinking about all that interracial marriage bullshit. Whites need to stick with whites and coloreds need to stick with coloreds."

"Damn right," Wally agreed.

Paul pretended to be busy arranging the stacks of papers on the counter. His Uncle Harry slowly made his way to the front of the store. He was walking with his cane. His movements were slower than they had ever been. Paul rose from his seat and offered it to his uncle. His uncle looked at all three and said in his dry, raspy voice:

"As you all know, your grandfather is in the hospital," he said. "We have to talk about who will be helping to run the family store. You've all been working here for years and know how to run things without much supervision. I'm getting up in my age as well and I'm in no shape to run the business. Wally, you are twenty-four and Paul will be hitting eighteen soon. If either of you would like to take over the store, you are free to do so. Your grandfather specifically wanted Paul to take over, but Paul has expressed that he didn't want the store. Isn't that right, Paul?"

"Yes," said Paul. "I have lived here all my life and I wanted to see what else is out there."

"What about you Wally?" Harry asked.

"I don't know, Pop," Wally said. "I just don't see myself wanting to stay in the store either."

"Why don't you ever let me run anything?" Bill demanded.

"You know damn well why," Harry said, staring blankly at him. "Everyone knows you don't care about the store. You break things too easily, give people back the wrong amount of change, don't clean up behind yourself, and scare all the women away. You embarrass the whole family with your erratic behavior. This store used to have tons of customers until you started working here. You ruined your grandfather's legacy with all your bullshit!" He grabbed his cane and angrily hit Bill with it. Bill cried out in agony and grabbed his leg as his father repeatedly beat him.

"Pop," Wally cried out, "It's okay, he doesn't want the store."

"Giving him the store was never an option," Harry said, eyeballing Bill. "Fucking dumbass is a worthless piece of shit. The whole town talks bad about us and this idiot is only making things worse. You better straighten up and you better do it now. This is your last warning from me before I have to break you myself."

He lowered his cane as another group of customers entered the store. Harry heatedly glared at Bill who was still holding his leg.

"What are you waiting for," Harry barked. "Get your fat ass out there and help them. Stupid piece of shit."

Bill lowered his head and slightly limped as he went towards the customers to assist them. Harry allowed no backtalk whatsoever when it came to matters of his household or dealings with Sal's. Now that Abraham was hospitalized, *his* word was law when it came to running the store. That was not the first time Paul and Wally had ever seen Harry beat Bill and Bill was not the only person he had beaten. The people that Harry truly hated made it into The Album and nobody was immune from it, including other family members whom the rest of the family had deemed disposable.

After Wally had given the customers back their change, Paul helped to carry the groceries out to the cars. The radio continued to talk about more and more protests. Harry gazed at the radio with abhorrence and tapped his cane at Wally.

"Turn that fucking radio off," he said. "I don't want to hear about those damn monkeys."

The bell to the store chimed and Paul reentered the store, this time followed by Henry. Henry greeted the Boudreaux family. It was that time again, for him to collect the money that his mother earned from her sales. Harry pulled out the tab notebook and kept a vigilant eye on the teen. Henry grabbed a nearby pen and signed the tab. Harry slammed the money onto the counter. A few coins fell to the floor reflecting his distaste for the teen.

"How are your parents?" Harry asked sardonically.

"They are well," said Henry. "My mother told me to tell you that she will be bringing a new batch of goods tomorrow and has been working on the new orders."

"I see," Harry said. "You do know that it's time we all need to renegotiate the terms of her sales. Your family has had more than enough time to keep the five percent fee. Your father has long returned to his job and the fee for sale items, such as hers in the store, is usually a thirty percent fee. If she wants to continue selling items here, she is going to have to pay the regular fee."

"I'll tell her," Henry said. Both exchanged extended stares before Henry left the store. Paul wanted to tell Harry that he wanted the Wilkerson family to keep the previously agreed upon fee as is. With Harry managing the store and him already expressing that he had no interest in keeping it, there was little that Paul could do about the transaction.

"Stupid leech," Harry mumbled, now reading a newspaper. The bell chimed again and a young white man, Richard Hawkins, stepped in. He was in his late twenties and came from another poverty-stricken family. He had a wife and a two-year-old son who lived three houses down from the Wilkersons. Mr. Hawkins took his hat off and approached Harry.

"Harry," he said, "I need to have a word with you. I lost my job recently and wanted to see if there was anything that I could do to earn a few dollars for my family. You know that I am a hard worker and am willin--."

"We don't have any openings," Harry said, resuming to read the paper.

"Anything would help," Richard begged. "My family has done business with your father before and we've always been true to our word. He can vouch for my family and I."

"You're not dealing with my father, you're dealing with *me*," Harry said. "Everyone in town knows that he has been hospitalized and is unable to make any more deals due to his health, which leaves me in charge, and I've spoken."

Richard's gaze fell upon Paul.

"Paul," he said, "please, talk to your grandfather—."

"Get out of my store!" Harry bellowed. "Paul doesn't make the decisions around here when it comes to the store, *I* do! You contact my father, you will live to regret it, you hear me!"

Richard rushed out of the store, leaving the Boudreaux family there alone once again. Wally took a deep breath and exhaled. For years, Abraham had always preached to the Boudreaux family about having a brotherhood and helping those who were in need, especially whites within the community. Regardless of how slow or great the store had been through the years, Abraham had always managed to find a way to help his race of people often calling his group of followers, The Family. Whether a person was a member or not, Abraham made deals, which increased its membership and loyalty onto him, whether future dealings were good or bad. A debt was owed and most had been paid back in full. Paul had been taught that, but some of his viewpoints had changed, and seeing his own uncle's viewpoints changing as well. He was beginning to even not help members of The Family, including members of his own household.

I don't know what to do, Paul thought. I could help so many people if I took my grandfather's place within The Family, but then I would have to give up the relationship that I've always needed in my life. I don't want to give up on the person who would never give up on me.

Chapter 22

Paul got out of the driver's seat of his car. Bill slightly limped out of the vehicle. Paul felt terrible for his cousin and had offered Bill ice earlier that day, but he refused. Bill, as usual, had that same angry, glower on his face as other students moved out of his way. Bill's eyes only softened when he noticed Nancy sitting on the bench with her friends in front of the school. Nancy smiled faintly as he approached her. Her eyes gazed at Paul, almost longingly as if to say she still wanted him back. However, they soon fell upon Bill with a bit of indifference. Paul greeted his friends.

"Well, I have to go," he said.

"Not this time," one of his friends said. "We never see you anymore in the mornings. We want to hang out like old times."

"Sorry," Paul said. "I can't." He eyeballed the parking lot, scanning for his girlfriend's car. She still hadn't arrived at the school.

"C'mon," his friend said, tossing his football at Paul. Paul caught the football and smiled. He tossed it back to his friend. Both teens soon began talking about the models of cars, western television shows, and the latest song on the radio. They were so engrossed in their conversation that Paul was shocked to hear the school bell ring. He scanned the parking lot and noticed that Nell's car was parked. He had missed their usual morning get together. Paul, who was guilt stricken, rushed into the school. He scanned the crowded hallway and saw no trace of her. He hurried to his locker and gathered his books.

Anxiously, he made it to his homeroom class and saw Nell sitting in her desk sorting her papers. Paul let out a small grunt of frustration and sat in his own desk. Minutes later, the bell rang again for the students to head to their first period class. Paul rushed to the math class and sat down. He hid a smile when Nell entered the class, taking her seat in the back of the classroom.

"Mr. Boudreaux," the teacher said, "could you take the liberty to help pass back yesterday's homework assignments?"

"Yes, sir," Paul said, taking the papers. He began to pass back the papers. His eyes fell upon Nell's who glanced at him questionably. As Paul handed her paper back, he lightly ran his finger across the back of her hand. He, then, passed back the other documents. When he returned Nancy's paper, she had a glimpse of uncertainty upon her face. This was a first for Paul. He questioned why she was giving him that strange look.

After class, Nancy waited for Paul to leave the classroom. Once he was out the door, she clutched his arm, startling him.

"Why did you brush *her* hand?" she inquired.

"What are you talking about?" Paul asked.

"Is there something going on between you and *Nell*?" she asked.

"No," Paul lied. "Why would you think that?"

"You brushed your hand against her hand," Nancy said, sounding outraged.

"You are imagining things, Nancy," Paul said. "I know that you are still upset about the breakup, but I don't have time to deal with this right now. We are both going to be late for class."

"Stop lying to me, Paul," Nancy said. "Is that the reason why you broke up with me was to be with *her*?"

Paul ignored her and walked to his next class. He was afraid that someone would find out about his secret relationship and over something as small as a light touch. He began to run thoughts in his mind on how to prevent Nancy from investigating things further. If she was going to dig for more information, he hoped that she would not go to Bill of all the people at the school. If Bill ever found out Paul's secret, then he would be regarded in an even worst light than him.

I have to throw off Nancy's suspicions, Paul thought. If she finds out, then not only will I be in danger, Nell will be too. I need to think of something fast. I know this is going to hurt her, but I have to do what I can to save our relationship.

After school, Paul was relieved to see Nell. He kissed her and locked the door. Nell was delighted to see him and took a place to sit on the empty teacher's desk. Paul sat next to her and held her hands.

"I'm sorry I missed you this morning," he said. "I lost track of time, please forgive me. Also, I have some bad news. Nancy is growing suspicious of us and we will have to stop seeing each other at school for a while. I don't want things to get out of hand."

"Then, how will we communicate or be together?" Nell asked. "This room is all that we have and if that is being taken away, we don't have anything anymore."

"I know," Paul said. "It's just until things get cleared. I can meet you this Saturday at 8 p.m., like last time."

"It's Monday," Nell said, her eyes filling with tears. "That feels like a long time from now."

"Babe, I know," Paul said, sadly. He embraced her and smooched her forehead. "It won't be long, I promise." He wiped the tears from her eyes with his hand. Trying to control his own emotions, Paul faced Nell again and kissed her, letting it linger. Gently, Paul pulled away. His thumb gently caressed the back of Nell's hand and Paul pulled his hand away. With a heavy heart, Paul left the room and walked down the hallway, alone.

Chapter 23

The week went by very sluggishly, with Paul sulking throughout most the week. He had become withdrawn from most activities at school and at work with the week dragging on. Unable to take the distance further, he eventually broke the break, meeting Nell the night before, getting the affection that he needed. Refueled, with contentment, Paul sensed his energy returning to him after the date. He had slept well that night and was awaken by a heavy enthusiastic knock at the door the next morning.

Making his way to the front door, Paul yawned. He combed his fingers through his hair and opened the door to find Henry on the other side. Paul rubbed his eyes and widened the door, letting his best friend inside. Henry laid on the couch and propped up an arm on the arm rest. Paul sat on a nearby chair, still half awake.

"What are you doing up this early?" Paul asked.

"Early?" Henry exclaimed. "It's almost 11 a.m. You should have been up a long time ago! Hurry and get dressed, we are going to go out and have some fun! I know you've been down lately about your grandfather being in the hospital and your breakup with Nancy."

"It's fine," Paul stretched. "I'm over it."

"Just hurry up and get dressed," Henry insisted. "We got to be somewhere in thirty minutes!"

Paul cracked a smile and jogged back upstairs. He washed up, brushed his teeth, fixed his hair, and got dressed.

He went back downstairs and found Henry watching the television. Henry turned off the tv set and both guys got into Henry's vehicle. Paul promptly braced himself as Henry's car squealed loudly when he pushed the pedal to the metal, sending the car flying down the street. Reminiscing old times, both guys jokingly howled out loud with excitement.

"Did you know that Brenda Miller has a thing for you?" Henry said. "Ever since she found out about you and Nancy being over, she's been asking about you. She's got huge tits and oh man, you should get over Nancy quick once you bury your head in those."

Paul turned red, gritting his teeth. He desperately needed to tell Henry that there no need for him to worry about his love life and that he was seeing a special girl, but both he and Nell had sworn their relationship into secrecy. Not even Henry knew, and if Paul had to bury his head into anyone's tits, it certainly wouldn't be Brenda Miller's.

"I don't have time for another girl," Paul said, wishing his buddy would take the hint.

Henry stopped his car in front of a modest looking house with cut grass, a white picket fence, and small bushes that were freshly cut. There was a car parked in the carport that was in fair condition with a little rust around the edges of the metallic décor. Henry blew his horn, and two figures came out of the house.

"You're not going to go up to the front door?" Paul asked.

"What for?" Henry said. "They aren't anyone special."

Paul swore under his breath as he got out of the passenger seat and into the backseat. Two girls from their high school greeted them as they got into the car. They both were cheerleaders from the same squad where Nancy was the captain. Paul recognized one of the girls, Doris Kelly, who was a fairly nice girl with an hourglass figure, red hair, and brown eyes. The other girl was Brenda Miller, whom was the more outspoken of the two with blonde hair and green eyes. Her teeth were slightly crooked, but hardly noticeable. Brenda sat next to Paul and Doris sat next to Henry. Henry drove them to the new popular roller-skating rink called Benny's Roller Skating. It had just opened a week ago, but even Paul had never been there before this time. The parking lot was filled, with Henry luckily taking the last unoccupied one, yards away from the building that was blasting with music and giving off an enthusiastic welcome.

Paul jammed his hands in his pockets, fidgeting with the handkerchief that Nell had given him weeks before as Brenda tucked her arm around his, following the other couple into the building. Inside, the teens waited in line behind several other eager teens, adults, and children. The roller rink was spacious, and a few teens were chuckling as part of the rink were being filled with people who were barely able to stand up with the roller skates on their feet. One little boy, who appeared to be about six years old, was crying while holding his mother's hand as she was encouraging him to have fun. A woman clutched into her date's arm, making him almost fall when he attempted to support both of them on his skates.

Unenthusiastically, Paul purchased tickets for himself and his "date" and Henry did the same with his. They found an empty table in the far corner of the rink and began to put on their skates.

"You will catch me if I fall, right Paul?" Brenda asked.

"Yeah," Paul muttered, somewhat still preoccupied in his own thoughts. *Nell is going to kill me if she ever finds out about any of this. Damn, Henry!* Paul adjusted his stance in the roller skates. This was his first time roller-skating and apparently the same for the other teens. Henry slowly went towards the rink, leaving his date behind with the other two. Steadying himself, he pushed forward onto the rink.

"Henry," Doris called out, "wait for me!"

But Henry was already yards away. Upset, Doris lingered behind with Paul and Brenda. A few people quickly swung past the teens. Entering the rink, Paul attempted to skate, but Brenda clenched his arm mirroring the little boy and his mother. Paul could barely skate with Brenda's death grip in his arm. Doris began to skate ahead of the lagging couple.

"Come on, you two are barely moving," Henry called out, skating past Paul and Brenda.

You would barely be skating if you had a rock attached to you too, Paul thought, irritated.

"I'm sorry," Brenda said, "I've never skated before."

"I'm not much of a skater either," Paul said. "But you can hold on as long as you need."

Brenda beamed. Slowly, she loosened her grip as they made a turn to the other side of the rink. By now, Henry and

Doris were skating with a little more ease and confidence. Doris had caught up to Henry who was still disregarding her, skating as if they weren't even together. Other couples were skating together, holding hands. Paul wished that he would be doing the same with Nell. She might have liked going to such a fun place. Paul imagined her holding his hand as they skated around the rink, smiling at one another, maybe laughing if they almost fell like some of the other couples were doing.

Getting closer to the entrance of the rink, Paul saw that Henry and Doris were back at the table. Henry nodded towards Paul and Brenda and took off, leaving Doris alone. Paul and Brenda sat down at the table and Henry returned with some food and drinks.

"We were talking about coming back next weekend," Doris said. "Skating is more fun than I thought. Then Brenda could *allow* Paul to skate. You two would make such a wonderful couple."

Paul nearly choked on his drink. The soda almost went down the wrong pipe, making him cough erratically. Brenda was cute, but he had no intention of ever being in a relationship with her or any other girl except Nell.

"What do you say, Paul?" Brenda asked.

"Um, no," said Paul.

Brenda's smile tanked into a low frown. Doris bit her bottom lip, embarrassed for her friend. Brenda cleared her throat and excused herself from the table. She rushed into the ladies' bathroom. Doris followed her friend, leaving the two teen boys alone. Unfazed, Henry continued to take gulps of his soda. Things were uncomfortable, especially hearing the shrieks of disappointment coming from the bathroom which was not far from the table.

"Calm down, Brenda," Doris could be heard saying. "He's just broken up with Nancy. I told you that it was too early to try to go on a date with him! He's not that good looking anyway."

Soon, both girls exited the bathroom, reappearing back at the table. Brenda's makeup was sightly smeared, and she had a handful of tissue in her hands, pressing them against her face, still bawling her eyes out.

"Henry, could you take us home?" Doris asked. "We are ready to go."

"I'm not going anywhere," Henry replied. "We just got here and I'm going to get my money's worth."

"That is so selfish of you, Henry," Doris snapped back. "Can't you see that Brenda is upset? We have to get home."

"Then walk home."

"You are so rude, Henry! No wonder the other cheerleaders don't like you!"

"You think I care about what you skirts think?" Henry stated. "If you're not going to finish your hotdog and drinks, I'll take them." He grabbed the remainder of their food and started to stuff his mouth. Livid, Doris stood akimbo.

"Well, aren't you going to say anything, Paul?" Doris demanded turning his way.

"I'm not arguing with my ride back home," Paul muttered.

Both girls seemed miserable while they all sat down and waited for Henry to finish eating what was left of his food and everyone else's. Once he was ready to go, everyone returned the skates and retreated back to Henry's car. Neither girl spoke on the ride back home and stomped out of the vehicle as soon as Henry parked the car back at Brenda's place. That was the one of the worst double dates both guys had been on in a long time. It was not unusual for Henry to make his date angry, but Paul's dates usually ended better. This time, his date was just as bad, even though it was not a date he had intended on going on in the first place.

"What's with you?" Henry asked. "Don't tell me you're still sour over Nancy. Why'd you break up with her if you still wanted her to be your old lady? She doesn't even like that neanderthal cousin of yours."

"It's not Nancy."

"Your grandfather?"

"No."

"Then what is it? You're never this secretive. You don't hang out with the guys anymore. You even turned down a girl with a nice rack. What's the deal?"

"Don't you ever get tired of the way that things are around here? I'm tired of being in The Family and having things falling on my shoulders all the time. I'm just done with it all and I don't see myself wanting to be in it, even after my grandfather passes. All it has ever done was create a division between everyone in the community. My own family hates me, even when I told them that I didn't want to take all my grandfather's assets and would share things with them."

"Yeah, but what can you do other than go along with it?" Henry pulled out of the driveway and began the drive again, driving slowly. "My family owes your grandfather so much money that we are barely keeping our heads above water. Lots of people are indebted to him. At least you were good enough to my family to give us a low interest rate. Most of the others here are at least thirty or more."

"Yeah, but it's stupid," said Paul. "If nobody had to pay all those dumb fees, they would be able to catch up."

"I'd rather it be you to take over instead of Harry or Wally any day," Henry said. "When Wally was being mentored, he'd make some people pay with forty percentage or more. Talk about greedy."

Paul wanted to tell Henry that if he could, he would completely forgive all the money that his family owed. They would have still been loyal towards the Boudreauxs. They had been, even before they fell upon hard times. The Family had been a well-constructed scam, in Paul's opinion, to gain money and power within the community. His grandfather held even more power than any judge, police officer, or mayor within the town.

"If anyone is going to have such power, it's going to be me," Abraham told Paul years ago. "He who yields the most power controls the masses."

Chapter 24

There was a loud commotion at the high school the following Monday. Nancy had found out about the double date and was on a rampage. She found Brenda and the two girls began fighting on the outside of the school where the teachers had to pull the girls apart and take them to the principal's office. Paul was relieved that nobody knew about his real new girlfriend but hoped that she too wouldn't get upset with him about the double date that he never intended to go on. Despite Nancy's wrath, other girls continued to go out of their way to gain Paul's attention by smiling, flirting, and trying to talk to him excessively. Even girls who had boyfriends wanted his attention and to be his rebound. Paul had no choice but to warn Nell about the unavoidable occurrence that was happening at the school. Anxious, Paul entered the science room to see Nell sitting with her back to him. Paul locked the door behind him, knowing that she too had learned about the double date. Paul sat down next to her, silent and prepared to endure any fury she would place upon him. Nell didn't face him, peering at the clouded sky that was now a reflection of her heart ache. Nell wiped a tear away with her hand, but failed to catch another as it immediately fell upon her modest yellow dress.

"I didn't cheat on you, Nell," Paul said. "I was supposed to be hanging out with Henry and he surprised me with the double date. I didn't even do anything with the girl, honest."

Nell's chest quivered as she failed to avoid crying more. Paul got out of the chair and put one knee to the floor, crouching in front of her. He grabbed her hand and kissed it.

"Nell, believe me, I love you," he said. "I never planned to go out with her. I only want you."

"Then why didn't you leave?" Nell asked.

"How could I leave when we all took Henry's car? You know how hardheaded he is! Nell, I promise you that I don't want any other girl. Henry set up the entire thing."

"What did you do with the other girl? Did you kiss her?"

"I didn't do anything with her! I haven't kissed another girl since we've been together."

"I don't know, Paul. There are other girls that are flirting with you."

"That's because they think I am single."

"Then stop telling people that you are!"

"Darn it, Nell! You know I can't do that! Just trust me and that I would never do anything to jeopardize our relationship. Next time someone tries to set me up on a surprise date, I will just leave. Even if I have to walk one hundred miles to get away, I will leave."

The bell rang. Paul lifted himself slightly and kissed Nell.

"I only love and want you, remember that," Paul rose to his feet and walked out of the classroom. He ran his fingers through his hair and grumbled. He avoided looking at any of the other students as he stormed into the homeroom classroom. He wished that Henry never would have set him on that dumb double date, but at least everyone knew that he didn't make out with Brenda. He had dodged a huge bullet with that one.

Both Nancy and Brenda entered the classroom covered in scratches from their quarrel earlier that day. Their hair was in disarray with Nancy trying to run her fingers through hers to groom herself. Bill scowled at Brenda, calling her an insensitive slur as she made her way past him to the other side of the classroom. Nancy avoided gazing at Paul, immediately opening her math book. Paul felt a tug on the back of his shirt. Someone was trying to pass him a note. Paul took the folded note from his classmate's hand and began to read it.

Want to make out?

Paul scowled, scanning the classroom. It was a note from a girl named Patty Manson. She winked at him. Uninterested, Paul scrunched up the paper, rolled his eyes, and tossed the paper away from himself. His heart began to race once Nell entered the drama filled classroom. Paul stared straight ahead to the board, wishing that the school day would hurry up and end. As bad as things were getting, even visiting his grandfather would have been a less dramatic situation. Tensions were high throughout the class with various people glaring and staring at each other. Luckily, not much was said for the rest of the class.

"What are you going to do?" Henry asked Paul during lunch. "All these girls are practically throwing themselves at you. The only one who isn't is that colored girl. I didn't think one double date would cause all of this. Did you hear that there was going to be a meeting in two days about this new business that is trying to pop up on the other end of town?"

"So what; businesses pop up all the time," Paul said, eating the last of his meal. As long it wasn't a threat, the new business would be safe from any wrath done by members of The Family. The last thing that Paul wanted to be a part of was another unnecessary attack.

"It's a colored business," Henry added. "A few of us plan on trying to stop it before it becomes a thing here. If one pops up, then others will come. You should be more concerned; they might even try to take away your family's business as much as some of these sympathizers are acting."

"All they do is start problems wherever they go," another jock whispered. "I bet they are waiting for the perfect time to riot in our school."

There they go again with all this paranoid talk, Paul thought. It's funny how everyone is threatened by the colored people in this community when people in The Family like to go around extorting money while burning and killing people. Heck, the idiots that they are following and worshipping can't even get their own families to get along! Why haven't they realized that they are no better off than the colored people if they were viewed as threats too? They make me sick with all this dumb shit. This has got to stop!

"There aren't even enough of them to start a real riot," Paul muttered. "We outnumber them anyway. We only have *two* in our grade."

"For now," Henry added. "I bet once their population gets big enough, they will try to take over everything and run all of us out of town. We need to take them out before it gets out of hand."

Paul wasn't surprised by the conversations from his group of friends. It was fairly common with them talking their paranoias about other groups of people taking over their small community. He hadn't heard of the new business, but then again, he had been distancing himself from his friends and other members of the community at a steady pace. He knew that people like Nell posed no threat. In fact, none of the Negro students had involved themselves in any of the drama that was being impacted by the school or community. They mainly kept to themselves, only wanting peace that was not being given to them by the mistrust and paranoia of others.

After school, Paul managed to sneak away and enter into the science room where Nell was waiting. He locked the door behind himself.

"Nell," he said, "I have to go to the hospital to visit my grandfather. I'm sorry; I can pick you up later tonight if you'd like."

"I understand," Nell said.

Paul gave her a quick smooch on the lips and exited the room. He went back out into the parking lot where Henry was searching the lot for him.

"Where'd you run off to?" Henry asked.

"I forgot something in my locker," Paul said, opening the door to his vehicle. "Let's get out of here. I got to visit my grandfather." He drove down the street, ending where the hospital stood. Reluctantly, Paul and Henry entered the facility where Henry soon took off to visit his cousin who worked as a nursing assistant there. Paul did his long walk down the corridor until he reached the room where Abraham was being kept. Paul knocked on the door and waited.

"Come in," Abraham's barely audible voice called out.

Paul entered the room and saw the man that was deemed the most feared in town. The elderly man had the sheets up to his chest. He was thinner than before, breaking Paul's heart. His height still tall in the bed. His eyes peered upon Paul, glassy and weak. The room had a small assortment of flowers given from various families. Paul sat down in an empty chair and the man cracked a smile.

"Paul," he said, "I must be dreaming. You are here?"

"I am," said Paul. "Sorry, I've been absent. There has been a lot going on---."

"Say no more," his grandfather said. "I was young once and know the pressures of a youthful life. Tell me, Paul...How is your uncle treating you and the other members of the community?"

"Fine, I guess. No different than before."

"I'd expect that from them," his grandfather said. "But, don't trust them. I've known people long enough to stay several steps ahead of them, especially from my own son. Your father was a brilliant man, Paul, but even he couldn't survive the traps that most people had for him. I tried to teach him as much as I could, but even I failed to prevent his death, including your mother's. Do you like Wally?"

"He's okay, but no different from the rest."

"He's different alright. He is the main one you need to keep an eye out for. His real father had to be disciplined by me. His father wanted your mother, despite having his own wife and child. Your father and him fought until one day, Wally's father had to be killed off because no matter how much we had to discipline him, he was always obsessed with your mother. His own wife took her own life, sorrowful that her husband desired another woman. I would not be surprised if he were plotting in the shadows, especially being raised by Harry who is upset that I am leaving everything to you."

"I don't want anything; I can take care of myself."

"Whether you want it or not, I am giving it to you. I consider you to be the only true family that I have left."

Chapter 25

Paul picked up a rock and tossed it into the swamp. The darkness and frog croaks reminded him of the area surrounding the family cabin, a place his uncle and cousins frequented. It still belonged to Abraham and would be one of many properties passed down to Paul. Paul had been to the cabin occasionally, but never enjoyed it much. It was an eerie location and he yearned for a less dismal place. Nell sat down by his side as the calm wind surrounded them. She placed a hand on Paul's thigh and squeezed it gently.

"You seem to have something on your mind, what is it?" she asked.

"Family problems," said Paul. "Nell, what do you think of families that only care about objects and not each other? Is that even a real family?"

"It's a family, but a bad one," Nell said. "My family may not have much, but we care about each other. My little sister, Claudine, drives me crazy every now and then, but I still love her and I'm sure that she loves me."

"You sure you don't have any doubts about your family loving you?"

"I'm *certain* that they love me. What about you and your family? Have things gotten better or worse since you tried to work things out with them?"

"My parents died a long time ago," Paul said. "But I'm sure that they loved me when they were still alive. I was raised by my grandfather who always told me to not trust anyone but him. Sure, I have my uncle and cousins, but we aren't close at all. My aunt is okay, on the rare occasions that I see her. Everyone hates each other, but only tolerates one another because of my grandfather. I tried to get along with everyone, but I still can't find myself fully trusting them and I'm sure they feel the same way about me. Since my grandfather is in bad shape, once he passes, I won't have anyone. I wish it didn't have to be like this."

"You still have me and your other friends, Paul. Like they say, sometimes your friends treat you better than your biological family. Your friends are the family that you choose."

Paul smirked at the irony and corruption of such a word: family. His own biological family and participants had all but corrupted the word, family, to him. It was nothing more than a team effort to hurt undeserving citizens with hopes of being the lead in a somewhat herd mentality. His grandfather hoped that he would take over as the head, who didn't even trust nor truly care for the rest that followed. Why would he even want to be part of such a twisted community?

"I don't even know who I am anymore," Paul said. "I am so confused and don't know what to think!"

Nell pulled her legs up to her chest. She tilted her head to the side and placed a comforting hand on Paul's back.

"Just be you," she said. "Just be Paul Boudreaux."

"Yeah, the pretentious person everyone thinks he is..."

"I don't think you're pretentious. If anything, you're a kind and loving person with good intentions. I wish more people were like you."

"*Why* do you love *me*, Nell?" Paul asked. He plucked a piece of grass from off the ground and bent it. *She certainly doesn't deserve to be sneaking outside of the house to be with the likes of me. A real gentleman would have braved it all and at least ask her parents' permission to date her. Sure, they could have declined my wish, but at least I would have given Nell and her family the same respect as I had given white girls in the past. I'm such a coward! But, if I did, what would it also mean for them, to know that their daughter was dating the grandson of a prejudiced killer and businessman? Maybe Nell would have been better off dating someone else.*

"I guess I'm still waiting to get back at you for old times sake," Nell joked.

Paul frowned.

"Kidding," said Nell. "I love you because you are kind, fun, and mean the world to me. I will admit that I didn't like you at first because you were disrespectful, but the more I got to know you, the more I realized what an amazing person you were and wanted to be yours."

"Not Martin's?"

"You're still jealous of him?!"

Paul smirked and pulled her closer to him. Sure, he was still jealous about Martin or any guy who would try to take Nell away from him. Who was Martin to ask her to the sock hop?

She was Paul's girl. The problem was that she wasn't welcomed to the sock hop or anywhere else within the school. She wasn't to be a part of them and their fun although Paul wanted to bring her deeply in his heart. Paul rose to his feet and turned up the radio in his car. Turning around, he helped Nell to her feet.

"May I have this dance?" Paul asked, cocking a smile.

"Sure, I promise I won't step on your feet as much this time."

"Step on my feet as much as you like. It will just remind me of how much I need to do better as a teacher," Paul pulled her closer, swaying to the sound of the music. It was a soft, romantic tune, reminiscing to him of how much she meant. Her missteps were just a sweet kick of spice, like her personality that would catch him off guard occasionally. He adored those moments, wishing for them often. The radio station switched to a faster paced song and soon it was Paul's turn to surprise her. He pulled away, extended his arm, and bringing Nell back closer to him. Naturally, she giggled nervously, but he knew that she liked it as much as he did. Now doing The Swim, Paul and Nell roared with laughter mimicking forward strokes and back strokes with their arms while swaying their bodies. That was a dance style that Paul knew that Nell liked, along with The Twist and The Mashed Potato. They were also his favorite dances which he liked to incorporate his own flirtatious moves. Nell laughed uncontrollably when Paul pretended to "swim" towards her, only to grab her by the waist and planting as many smooches onto her neck as he could. Hardly able to contain her laughter, Nell ran towards the trees with Paul pursuing her. Being the faster of the two, Paul caught Nell from behind, elevating her off the ground. Again, he teasingly planted more kisses on her neck quickly before letting her go once again. Turning around, Nell lightheartedly sent a playful jab onto his shoulder.

As much as Paul wanted the night to continue, it was getting late. Both teens returned to the car, driving back to Nell's home and the secret meeting place. Paul parked the vehicle across the street. Woefully, he watched as Nell once again headed to her window.

"To heck with it all," he muttered to himself, getting out of the vehicle to follow her. Nell opened her window and climbed inside, unaware of Paul shadowing her. Reaching to lower the window, Nell let out a surprised gasp, seeing Paul out of the car and by the window.

"What are you doing here?" Nell asked.

"Kissing you goodnight," Paul whispered, leaning forward. Pressing his lips against hers, his heart began to race, filling the thrill of it all. Tonight, wouldn't be the time for more fun and he was getting tired. *Maybe next time.* Paul gave her a quick wink and headed back to the car waiting for him across the street.

Chapter 26

The following evening, surprisingly, Paul had been invited to return to his uncle's home for what would have usually been a monthly get together at one point in time. He had been invited by Harry, whom was not in as much of a sour mood as he had been previously. In good faith, Paul agreed to attend the dinner. Unfortunately, Bill had invited Nancy, who was sitting directly across the table from Paul. Her eyes avoided Paul's as she dug into her slices of roast beef. Bill was in good spirits. Normally, he would be sitting down stuffing his face and chewing with his mouth open, but ever since he started dating Nancy, he had been making great efforts to improve his once disgusting table manners. Most of the family had already known about Nancy dating Paul previously, but she had never been invited to the dinners until that day.

"So, what do you think about the roast beef, Nancy?" Bill's mother, Henrietta, asked.

"It's delicious," said Nancy, forcing a smile. "One of the best I've ever had. I must get the recipe."

"Our family has a recipe book," Henrietta said. "I'll be sure to write everything down for you."

Paul tightened his grip to his fork. He felt the slight brush of a foot rubbing against his leg from under the table. The foot traveled up his leg, forcing him to silence a moan that almost escaped his lips. He used his leg to push away the foot, but no matter what he did, it would always come back. Finally, Paul looked at Nancy, who was trying to hide a grin. She quickly took a drink of water from her glass and licked her lips before finally looking at him for a moment. Then, she smiled innocently at her hand which was being held by Bill.

"What are your future plans for when you finish high school, Nancy?" Henrietta asked.

"I plan on going to school to become a high school principal," said Nancy. "I need to get more experience by being a teacher first, but I would like to stay here in Wood Oak. I love this community and want to give back as much as I can." She once again moved her foot up Paul's leg.

"That sounds lovely," Henrietta said. "Bill is so lucky to have such a caring and community-oriented girlfriend."

"Excuse me," Paul said, rising from the table. He had enough of Nancy's games. He quickly walked to the bathroom. His heart was racing. He turned on the sink and filled his cupped hands with water. He dug his face into the water, hoping to relieve himself. He was upset with his ex-girlfriend. She was still trying to flirt with him and in the presence of his family. If Bill or the others ever found out, they would be greatly upset, and the last thing Paul wanted was for there to be another excuse for his family to despise him more. Paul knew that Nancy wanted to be in control. She had lost her power over him, but she still had Bill, who was a walking time bomb. Paul began to fear that she would use Bill to turn against him, making Paul wish that Bill would have chosen someone else to fall in love with and not her. He knew that he had enough drama to deal with, without Nancy and Bill. Paul's heart jumped at the knock of the door. He quickly dried his face with a towel and opened it. To his horror, it was Nancy. With a mischievous twinkle in her eye, she pushed him back and quickly closed the door behind her. She stepped forward trying to embrace him, but Paul stepped back further.

"I want you back, Paul," she said, anguish in her voice. "I miss us and what we had. Don't you want me too?" She tried to lean forward to kiss him. Paul backed away, avoiding her advances.

"I told you that we were through," Paul said. "We aren't together anymore. You are dating Bill. Why can't you just do this with him?"

"I don't want that smelly, fat, pig," Nancy said, with revulsion. "He is rude, filthy, and swears like a pirate. I only got with him to make you jealous. Don't you miss me? I miss you. We were good together and I can't see myself ever being happy with anyone else except you. If you will take me back, I will dump Bill and we can start over."

Paul frowned and Nancy's eyes were frantic, almost brimming with tears.

"I am sorry," said Paul. "I don't have plans on us ever getting back together. I just want to move on. If you don't love Bill, maybe it would be a good idea to be honest with him and not waste his time. He seems to really like you and you just using him to get back at me is not fair to him. We've already had this discussion many times about how you shouldn't pretend to be nice to others, to have your way, only to mistreat them later. You know that I hate that and yet you are doing it to my cousin this time."

"I never did it to you."

"You shouldn't do it to anybody," said Paul, walking past her and opening the door. He walked away, leaving her in the bathroom still upset. Walking in the hallway, he saw that the rest of the family was now in the living room listening to his aunt play the piano. He noticed that Bill was scanning the room for Nancy and only calmed down once he spotted her walking into the room. She appeared to be saddened but gave him a quick pretentious smile. Bill beamed and held her hand in his. His giant hand almost hid her hand completely. She whispered something into his ear and his eyes lit up. Soon, both of them left the room together. Paul was relieved. She was gone for now.

"Are you going to the cabin this weekend, Paul?" Wally asked him.

"No," said Paul. "I have to work on a project for school."

"We hardly see you at the cabin anymore," Wally said. "Hunting isn't the same without you. I'd rather go with you, than that brute, Bill. All he does is talk about Nancy or go on his rampages. How did our family ever get such a disgraceful swine like him? I'm surprised that Nancy is even dating him. He might treat her well, but I don't think that she loves him as much as she did with you."

"Maybe she might grow to love him," Paul said, clearing his throat.

"Is that so?" Wally whispered, "You surprise me when you were alone with her in the bathroom."

"Nothing happened," Paul whispered. "She is the one who followed me."

"Do you want her back?"

"No, I don't want her."

"Do a better job at turning her down for good," Wally said. "Last thing we need is for there to be more of a conflict between family members. You know that isn't tolerated now that our grandfather found out that you've been coming back for dinner. You do know that half of the family is upset because you are Grandfather's favorite and he wanted to leave everything to you. You should watch out for Bill and that girl. They could cause you to have many unnecessary mishaps."

Paul knew better than to believe Wally's half-truths. Though Wally had periods of allegiance to Paul, like his grandfather, Wally had a tendency to have very limited loyalty and he had attempted to betray him years ago before Abraham disowned him. It was true that Paul should be careful of Bill and Nancy, but it was not just them, but Wally as well. Wally had been their grandfather's second favorite grandson. Throughout the years, Paul began to take more notice that Wally would try to pin most of his schemes on Bill, making Bill look more unfavorable in Harry's eyes. It had worked so well that Bill was now the laughingstock of the family. Wally was slyer and more ruthless than Bill who was more open about his emotions. Paul prayed that his grandfather would live longer. He had been the only one who had been protecting him the whole time, with the rest of the family obeying his will. His word was law. Once he passed, it was possible that Harry that would try to seize control and, like Bill, he was capable of anything.

Chapter 27

The week dragged on, but slowly, things were getting calmer around the school. Henry and a few of the guys began having more talks about the hunting season and the girls had become less aggressive with their attempts to persuade Paul into dating them. Since the season had been over for football, Paul had more time to think about the university he wanted to attend: The Semmes College in Michigan. It seemed to be a far enough place for him to go without worrying about his family and the members of his grandfather's organization. He could also openly be with Nell, should she be willing to leave with him. For the last few days after leaving work, Paul would immediately drive outside of town in search of an ideal place. Some buildings were nicer than others, but each time he would enter a building, he would recognize the managers or owners, meaning he would still have to look elsewhere. He needed to find a building that would be far enough yet owned and managed by someone unrecognizable or did not know him nor his family. It took three days for Paul to finally find a modest hotel about forty miles away from Wood Oak. He spent the next few days going back and forth each day, not recognizing any of the staff or patrons. Luckily, it was an integrated hotel, meaning that nobody would probably mind him bringing his girlfriend along.

"This will do," Paul said to himself, entering the hotel lobby. He booked a room in advance and continued his journey back towards Wood Oak. On his way back, he noticed a small flower shop. He parked his vehicle in a parking space and entered the building where an old woman sat. She said her greetings to him, and Paul browsed the store. There was such a nice selection of flowers that Paul was unsure as to which ones to give to his girlfriend. *Everything looked beautiful, but which one would be the best for her?* Paul knew that Nell liked yellow flowers, but yellow was a friend-type of flowers and she was more than a friend to him.

"Red roses are always the best," the old woman said, as if reading his thoughts.

"Hmmm," Paul said looking at his watch. *Darn!* He would have to leave soon. He asked the woman when the flower shop would be closed, and she said within the next two hours. That would still give him enough time to make up his mind. He rushed out the door and hopped into his car. Almost speeding, he drove back to Wood Oak as the sun began to set. He still had plenty of time to kill once he approached Nell's neighborhood. He parked in his usual spot and waited. Once Nell met up with him again, he did not tell her of his plans. He knew that she would be expecting for them to go to the drive-in or deep within the swamps, but instead he took the route he had planned. Parking the car in front of the hotel, he exited the vehicle and opened the back door. Holding Nell's hand, they both walked to the outside door of the hotel room. Inside, he instructed for her to wait for him and that he would be back soon.

Paul returned to the flower shop and purchased a small bouquet of red roses that were just as beautiful as his feelings for his girlfriend. A few minutes later, Paul returned to the hotel room and locked the door behind him again. He handed her the small bouquet of roses, bringing a smile to Nell's once worried face. He guided her towards the bed and they both laid down with Nell resting her head on his chest.

"We are in a room again, nobody will bother us here," he said.

"But a *hotel* room?" Nell said, laughing.

"We had to go somewhere to relax and be comfortable," Paul said. "It beats being in a cramped car or uncomfortable classroom. Look, we even have a nice television set to watch programs."

"Paul," Nell said. "I have to tell you something. Don't get mad."

"What is it?"

"My sister knows about us."

Paul let out a low groan.

"How'd she find out?" he finally asked.

"She said that someone she knew saw us and they told her," Nell said.

"Is she going to talk? Does anyone else know?"

"She said she won't tell anybody," Nell said. "I don't think anybody else knows except her and her friend."

"You know that Nancy has her suspicions," Paul said. "We have to be more careful than ever. We only have a few more months and hopefully we can get out of here. Nell, you asked me about secrets. If I tell you one, will you promise that it won't tear us apart?"

"What is it, Paul?"

"My family is extremely dangerous," he said. "We are part of the Klan and my grandfather is its highest-ranking member in Wood Oak. So far, he knows nothing of us and that is why we are safe for now. His words are that powerful and that is why so many fear him. My blood members are more feared than the non-blood members of 'The Family.' My cousin is not the only other member who goes to our school. There are several others there hiding in plain sight. That's why it's important for nobody to know about us. We could die; both of us. If you are scared of Bill, he is nothing compared to some of the others. The Klan is highly organized and brutal. If it had been Bill or Wally there with you in the rain that night, you wouldn't have been seen again. I have seen things that I still have nightmares about. I never meant to hurt you by not wanting to do certain things with you, but I am only trying to protect you because I love you."

"Then why are you not like them, if you lived with them all your life?"

"My mother wasn't brought up in it," Paul said. "She often kept her opinions hidden from my father and the rest. When both she and my father were still living, she would tell me to not say anything against them, especially since my father was my grandfather's favorite son. I just remained silent about how I felt as a means of survival. Anyone that 'The Family' hates, they take them back to the cabin and dispose of them. That's why I try to avoid going there if I can. Once 'disposable' people are taken there, it is pretty much over for them. It is a hunting ground, and several members are hunters while others deal with medical and judicial systems, making it easier to get away with their plans."

"But, if you are a favorite, why would anyone want to go after you?"

"It's the worst position to be in," Paul explained. "Because of that, all eyes are on me. My grandfather is dying and now any power or protections that he has for others will die with him. I am in a very vulnerable position and even though I get along with most people, they wouldn't hesitate to take me out once he is gone. He had willed several assets to me that others are desperate to get for themselves. Even though I have expressed many times that I do not want anything, I can still see all the hatred and jealousy in their eyes. In all honesty, I just want to leave this whole life behind."

Nell exhaled. Paul turned her way; his eyes were serious and relieved that he had finally confessed more to her. Yet there also was the question of how she would respond.

"It seems as though your life would be better without me in it," Nell said. "If we never would have gotten together, you would have less to worry about. You seem to already have a lot going on without adding our relationship into the whole scenario. If being with me means that your life is in that much danger, maybe we shouldn't be together."

"I already knew the risks before we got together," said Paul. "You make it sound like I think that you are a burden, and you are not. My life has gotten better with you in it. You are what keeps me going and someone who I can trust. You could have left me a long time ago and had nothing further to do with me, but you stayed. As you said, what girl in her right mind would want to go through all that you are going through to be with me? If anyone deserves my love and loyalty, it's you. Once we can get away from Wood Oak for good, I want to make a lot of things up to you. I want to give you all the love and attention that you deserve, freely and out in the open. I promise that I will do everything that I can to make you just as happy as you have made me."

"You are really promising me all of that, Paul?" asked Nell.

"I promise you," said Paul, delivering a gentle kiss to her lips. Nell smiled and returned his kiss. Paul wrapped his arms around her. Soon, they both were consumed in their passions.

Chapter 28

"Where is he?" Abraham asked.

"He said that he would be here shortly," Harry said, leaning forward with his cane.

There was a knock at the door before it opened. Paul walked inside and greeted both his uncle and his grandfather who was lying in the bed. His grandfather smiled faintly and turned to Harry.

"Leave us and go outside," the old man said.

With a gruff mutter, Harry sluggishly sauntered outside with the aid of his cane and closed the door behind him. Paul sat down in the chair that his uncle had sat in and glanced at the man who was the most feared by all in Wood Oak. He was no longer the tall and scary man whom most cowered upon sight. Now, he was frail and no longer threatening. Yet, what power he had left was still respected.

"You asked to see me, Grandfather," Paul said.

"Yes," his grandfather said, weakness in his voice. "I do not have much time left. I wanted to see you one last time and only you... I know that you do not want any of the assets, but I am still leaving everything to only you... It has already been sealed. What you need to do right now is to make sure that you do not underestimate your uncle and his sons. If you need to get rid of them, do not hesitate to do it quickly."

"Get rid of them?" exclaimed Paul. "I thought that we were not allowed to have any rifts in the family any longer. If I get rid of them, then that would be breaking our own rules."

"If you get rid of them, then you can become the head and make your own rules," his grandfather said. "I only put that in place to protect members like you while you were young. Harry and his sons will most likely go after you to get the assets whether you choose to lead or not. They are too greedy and irrational. With the money you inherit, you can get more loyalty from the others. They can be bought, and you will have enough."

"I have no plans on leading," Paul said. "I do not want to stay here. I want to start a new life outside of Wood Oak. If Harry and his sons want to have everything, they can have it."

"You can't leave 'The Family,'" his grandfather coughed. "There is no place to run or hide. The only way out is death. I am giving you the opportunity to take control. Harry is getting weaker, but his son Wally is smart and will do anything to make it to the top to fulfill his greed. Bill is physically strong but lacks intelligence. You are young, smart, and would make a good, fair leader. But goodness and fairness are weaknesses. You must learn to get rid of both if you want to deal with the others. Do not waste your potential."

"I do not want to lead a group of racist radicals," Paul said. "I don't want anything. I am leaving whether you want me to stay or not."

His grandfather chuckled and glanced at the ceiling of the room. He slowly took in a deep breath and exhaled.

"Then, I guess it will not be long until I see you again," he said, taking his last breath.

Chapter 29

With an uncanny uneasiness, Paul finished stacking the shelves. He was still haunted by his grandfather's words. Wally and Bill resumed their usual duties at the family store, under the supervision of Harry who sat behind the counter, smoking his pipe calmly. It appeared that things were going on as usual. Paul's grandfather had already had his funeral and was now buried, leaving the position of leader to Harry since Paul chose to not take it. There was still disgust and vulgar language given to store patrons who were not white, despite them being allowed to shop at the store.

"Aren't you going to bag the groceries?" a young Negro customer asked.

"Bag it yourself, you damn monkey," Bill snorted, walking away.

Angrily, the patron stuffed the groceries into the bag and took off.

"They know damn well they need to go somewhere else," Bill complained. "There are two other grocery stories down the street. Dumbasses."

"Shut your damn mouth," Harry said. "Last thing we need is for the state to get on us about not allowing them in. They can still shop here, but we don't have to respect them."

The door to the store opened and a tall, thin white man walked in with a young girl who looked no older than five. She had various bruises on her arms and legs and was unusually quiet for a child. The man purchased some bread and barked at the girl to follow him back to the car.

"Get in the car, Allison," he said, with a chilling tone in his voice.

Harry resumed to smoke his pipe and gawked at Paul.

"Paul," he said. "It looks like we are running low on the canned corn. Go out back and get some more to restock that other shelf."

Paul nodded and went to the supply room. Harry, then, glanced at his two sons and called them over to him. He stood up more firmly with his cane.

"You two do whatever it takes to get some dirt on Paul," he said.

"He is too much of a saint," Wally said. "And everybody likes him. It would have to be something extreme and not your average dirt to make anyone go against him. Do we really have to get rid of him? He did say that he was going to split the assets with you, and he already gave up his position as leader to you."

"What good is being a leader without many assets?" Harry said. "With the *full* assets I could be the ultimate powerhouse and I waited too long to have some punk kid snatch it up from my grasp. Darn old man gave him too much of an advantage. He has the financial means to turn everyone against us with the assets alone if he wanted to. People follow the money, not titles with no merit. I don't trust him to split anything. Add to the fact that he more liked than all three of us combined."

"Maybe people won't care about how much money he has nor defend him if they too have something to lose," Wally suggested, smirking.

"But nobody else has anything to lose," Bill said.

"There is always something to lose," Harry thought out loud. "Him being his grandfather's favorite, he knows a lot of dirt on several people and his grandfather used their fear to control them. With his word, money, and fear tactics, he could expose everyone, and they lose everything. Now that his grandfather is gone, we could use this as an opportunity for people to think that those secrets will die with Paul if he were gone for good. It would be to their advantage to help us. Otherwise, he could expose them. We just need something on Paul to push them in the right direction to set the plan into motion."

Chapter 30

A month had passed since the death of Paul's grandfather. Luckily for Paul, Nell had been one of his main supporters during that difficult time and Paul was making progress and finding more reasons to smile each day. Nell embraced Paul as he held her in his arms. He playfully lifted her up off the ground and spun her in a short circle before kissing her. Nell giggled and returned the kiss. It was nighttime again and there was a blanket on the ground in the woods that Paul had laid out. As they both sat down on the blanket, Paul wrapped his arms around Nell and laid her down onto the blanket as he continued to kiss her.

"I love you," he said between the kisses.

"I love you too," Nell said, smiling. "I have to tell you something, Paul."

"What is it?" Paul asked.

"I'm pregnant," Nell said.

Paul pulled away slightly, surprised.

"Are you sure, Nell?" he asked.

"Yes," she said. "I am late, and I've been slightly sick the past few weeks."

Paul sat up. He ran his hand through his hair, trying to take the news in. He smiled and looked back down at his girlfriend. Nell sat up, surprised to receive another kiss from Paul.

"We're going to be parents," he said. "I can't believe it. Us... I guess that means that I will have to marry you, not that I hadn't already planned to do so once we left here."

"Do you think we will be good parents?" Nell asked.

"Absolutely," said Paul. "You would make a great mother and you know that I would do everything in my power to make sure that you both are taken well care of."

"Once we leave Wood Oak, where will we go?"

"Anywhere, I guess," said Paul. "Even if we have to spin a globe and point to an area, we will go there."

"Seriously, Paul," said Nell, "where would we go?"

"Anywhere," he said. "I mean it, where would you like to go? We will go there and have our family. We have the means to take care of ourselves financially. I just want you to be happy."

"I heard that Detroit would be a good place to go," Nell said. "What do you think? It might be cold there, but anything beats Wood Oak."

"Then that's where we will go," Paul said, smiling.

"There's also one other thing, Paul," Nell said. "I still have to tell my parents about us and our baby. I know that you said not to, but maybe they won't do anything. I can't just disappear from their lives once we decide to leave."

Paul breathed deeply. He stared at the night sky as if conflicted in his own thoughts.

"Just give it a little more time, Nell," he said finally. "I don't want you to be taken away from me. Let's just wait a little longer before telling them. Right now, it's early and unnoticeable."

"Okay," said Nell. "I'll wait a little longer. What are you hoping that we will have?"

"It doesn't matter," said Paul. "I'll be happy with whatever we have, boy or girl."

"Well, I would like a girl," Nell said, smiling.

Paul grinned, wrapping his arm around her.

Chapter 31

"Are you sure that this is okay?" Nell asked, looking nervous. Once again, they were in the library. It had been a while since they were out in the open together, sitting side by side with books in front of them. Paul looked untroubled and poised.

"We are working on a group project, nobody will suspect anything," he whispered.

Soon, two other students sat down across from them with their books and poster boards. Paul took the role as the group leader, instructing each member of their duties. Every now and then, he would sneak a smile and wink Nell's way, teasing her.

"You have the best handwriting out of all of us, Nell," said Paul. "Would you like to help Veronica with the poster while Luke and I discuss what we are going to write for the paper, after we get more books?"

"Sure," Nell said, smiling. She waited as Veronica pointed out which sentences to add to the poster as she used her handwriting to decorate the poster. Soon, they both started to work on their decorative drawings.

"That looks amazing," said Veronica. "We might get the highest grade in the class!"

"We still have a few more days to work on it," said Luke. "I'll see if I can find more books on the Louisiana Purchase. Let's go, Paul."

Both Paul and Luke went to the card catalogue and found the locations of several books on the Louisiana Purchase. Luke and Paul began grabbing arm loads of books, finding more than what they had expected. Returning to the table, Paul noticed that Veronica was alone. He squinted his eyes questionably but sat down with the other two students. He opened one of the books and began to scan for information when he heard the library door reopening. Nell approached the table with a frown. Paul observed that she had an arm wrapped around her stomach.

"I'm sorry," said Nell. "I have to go home. I don't feel well."

"But we were just getting started," Veronica complained.

Paul shushed her and glanced at Nell, concerned.

"If you don't feel well, then it would be best if you went home, Nell," he said. "I'll see you to your car." Luke and Veronica gazed at each other as Nell grabbed her things. Paul pushed his seat in and walked out the door with Nell to her car.

"I'm sorry, Paul," she said. "I just haven't been myself the last couple of weeks. I just can't keep much down, and I just feel weak every now and then."

"I know, Babe," Paul whispered. "I'm sorry that you don't feel well. I wish that there were more that I could do to make you feel better." He looked around briefly before grabbing her hand and giving it a little squeeze. He sighed deeply before letting her hand go. His eyes were apologetic. "I'll come tonight and see you."

"Okay," Nell said, getting into her car. She glanced at Paul from the window, knowing nothing more could be done. She kissed her hand and pressed it against the window. Paul smiled. He kissed his hand and pressed it against her hand on the window. Nell started her car and drove away.

Paul returned to the library and continued to work on the group project until closing time. It had been a long day and unfortunately, he would have to return to Sal's. Tired, he reluctantly went to the store and began his usual duties of stocking shelves and assisting with the customers. Harry, Bill, and Wally were unusually quiet.

"Why don't you take the rest of the day off, Paul," Harry said. "I'm going to close the shop early today."

"Really?" said Paul. It was unusual for the store to close early, but then again, Harry was now in charge. Maybe he was going to be more relaxed with the rules, unlike Abraham who had been stricter. Paul finished stocking the last canned item and signed out. Now that he could leave earlier, he could check on Nell and see if her condition had improved. Leaving the store, he returned home, took a quick shower, and put on a new fresh set of clothes. He waited for the clock to reach his usual meeting time. At 7:45 p.m., he hopped into his vehicle and drove to the spot where he usually parked near Nell's place.

He waited for a vehicle to drive past him into the dark, before crossing the street to Nell's window. Lightly, he tapped on the window and she opened it for him. Enthusiastically, Paul greeted her with his array of playful kisses.

"My Nell, are you okay, Babe?" Paul asked, climbing inside.

"I'm still sick," Nell said. "I was barely able to eat anything. Some of the smells made me feel worse."

"I'm sorry," Paul said. This was the first time he was ever in her room. He sat down on the bed next to her and wrapped his arm around her. "So, this is your room..." He looked around, beaming.

"Yeah," said Nell, "It's small, but at least I don't have to share a room with Claudine. She is so nosey. I'm surprised that she is not snooping around here right now. Where is your car?"

"I parked it out on the street," said Paul. "There are other cars parked there. Maybe it will just blend in with the rest."

"I'm glad that you came," Nell said. "But I don't want you to get in trouble for meeting me here. My parents are pretty strict about everything. I don't even want to think about what would happen if they found a boy in my room."

"Yeah," Paul laughed. "Well, since my grandfather passed, his house is empty, and nobody will disturb us there. We could go there once you feel better. It's pretty isolated and I could pick you up tomorrow night, if you want to go. We could spend more time together. We could even try to come up with names for our baby."

"I'd like that," Nell said.

"I'll see you then," Paul said. He kissed her before going back out the window. Before crossing the street, a car zoomed past Paul, barely missing him. Taking a step back, Paul tried to make out the car but couldn't in the darkness. Maybe it was some drunk or something. Paul shook his head and got back into his car. It had been a long day and he needed to get some much-needed rest.

Chapter 32

Paul couldn't be happier. Harry had called him earlier the next day, stating that he could take the day off and that he, Wally, and Bill would be out of town for the weekend. With a full day to himself, Paul could finish his schoolwork and possibly have more free time to do what he wanted. He quickly focused on his homework assignment. The topic for the English assignment was to describe the happiest day of his life. Paul knew what his answer was: finding out that he was going to become a father. He wanted to write about how he wanted to marry Nell and raise their family in a peaceful and welcoming environment, free from hiding in the shadows. He wanted to embrace the ones he genuinely thought of as family to him and hold them as tightly as he could. However, Paul knew that he could not write that essay, as much as he wanted. At least, not until he was free, and the time was not now. Woefully, he began to write about something trivial such as winning a football game and making a touchdown. One day, he hoped that he could verbalize and express his truths about Nell.

Later that night, once again, he met up with Nell. Knowing that his uncle and cousins were out of town, he could take his girlfriend home with him and not some hotel or wooded area. She would be his welcomed guest and be in another part of his world.

"Are you feeling better, Babe?" he asked.

"A little," said Nell. "How far are we driving this time?"

"Just a few more blocks and we should be there," Paul said happily. "You can now come inside since the only person who will be living there is me for now. Once I graduate, I'm going to sell it. No use on keeping a house here when we both plan to leave to go to Michigan."

He parked the car and they both walked to the back entrance of the house. Nell looked at it in amazement. It was big and beautiful. Paul unlocked the door to the home and held Nell's hand as they both walked inside. He locked the door and turned on the lights. Playfully, he lifted Nell off her feet and spun her around like he usually would and planted a kiss on her lips.

"My beautiful Nell," he said. "I can't wait for us to be married and have our baby."

Suddenly, the door burst open, surprising them. Paul pushed Nell behind him and was surprised to see his uncle and cousins pointing their rifles at them. Paul stood sternly in front of Nell, who was now shaking in fear. *How did they find out? Where did they come from? They were supposed to be out of town!*

"Stay behind me, Nell," Paul said, his voice panicked.

"So, *this* is what you were hiding, boy," Harry said, striking him with his cane.

Paul fell over from the blow and grabbed his left leg. He cried out in pain as blood began to bleed through his pants leg. Nell screamed in horror as Wally grabbed her by the arm and held her firmly. Bill pointed his rifle at Nell.

"Shut up," Harry said, smacking Nell across the face. Nell fell to the side from the impact of the strike.

"Leave her alone!" Paul shouted, trying to rise to his feet. He cried out in agony as he struggled to get up. Harry struck him again, forcing him back down to the floor.

"Take them to the truck," Harry ordered his sons, who forced both Nell and Paul to follow them. Once everyone was in the back of the truck, Harry drove them to a dark desolate area. There were dark trees with Spanish moss hanging from them. To Paul's horror, he knew where they were being taken to, the cabin. He looked helplessly at Nell as the car stopped in front of the cabin. Light glowed from the inside of the cabin, like the bright, ominous eyes of a dark entity staring down at them. They were not alone with their kidnappers. There were other people there gathered on the outside of the swampy, wooded area holding lamps, flashlights, and rifles. The sound of crickets and frogs bellowed with the sounds of people chattering as they approached the parked truck. Paul recognized their faces. It was "The Family." There were doctors, lawyers, teachers, judges, students, and many others of all ages from the very young to the very old. Harry removed the keys from the truck as Wally and Bill forced Paul and Nell out of the back of the truck. Harry stood before them, leaning on his cane.

"As you all can see," Harry said, "your beloved Paul is seeing this colored girl. We found them both at my father's house, together. He has been sneaking around seeing her from right under our noses. He has plans on taking *all of us* down before running off with her. He does not have any of your interests at heart. You can see which race of people he is loyal to. He certainly doesn't care for any whites when he is in bed with a damn monkey."

Paul and Nell stared in horror as many eyes fell upon them. There were many whispers and looks of disgust. Husbands were talking to their wives. Mothers were talking to their children. Siblings talking to each other. He even spotted a few classmates, including Henry and a few members of the football team who were dumbfounded. Henry broke eye contact with Paul. He hanged his head low and disappeared into the crowd, leaving his best friend. Paul curled his lip and stood up, weakly. The pain from his leg radiated, but he fought back to ignore it.

"That's not true," Paul shouted. "I never had any plans on taking anyone down. If that were true, wouldn't I have already done that by now?"

"But is it true that you are seeing *her*?" someone from the crowd asked.

Paul's eyes met Nell's. Her face was blooded and covered in tears. She lowered her head, defeated. Easily, Paul could lie to everyone and deny ever being involved with her. He could say that she was just a classmate and nothing more to him. Paul took in a deep breath. He was tired; tired of hiding in the shadows; tired hiding whom he wanted to be with. Paul swallowed hard and finally he spoke, raising his head.

"I *am* seeing her," he confessed. "She is no less than any other woman out here! She is smart, beautiful, and is a wonderful person. Neither she nor I had any plans on bringing any harm to anyone out here. We love each other and just want to live our lives openly. Whatever any of you want, you can have, we just want to be left alone."

"That's disgusting," someone shouted.

"I can't believe it," another person said. "He really *does* like coloreds more than whites. No wonder he dumped his white girlfriend."

"Him seeing her is proof that what we are saying is true," Harry announced. "If he were hiding the fact that he was seeing her, what more could he be hiding? He managed to con my father into giving him everything, leaving the rest of us penniless. If he is doing this to his own blood, imagine what he has in store for the rest of you. He has dirt on every one of you. This will be your *only* opportunity to get rid of him once and for all."

"He has never done anything to go against any of us before," a young man said.

"But he is a high risk if we let him go," an older person said. "He would be better off dead, and he also has that girl who now knows about us. Our livelihoods and families are at stake."

"It is either him or you and your families," said Harry. "Are you willing to sacrifice everything for him and his colored mistress or are you going to finally be free of any future blackmail, threats, or arrests? The choice is yours. As your leader, I say it would be in everybody's interest to dispose of him *and* her."

"I've never done anything against any one of you," Paul snapped back. "I never conned my grandfather into giving me anything. Anything he gave to me; he gave freely of his own will. I've never been greedy for power nor money. All of you know that! I have no desire for any of it. I just want to have a chance to be with the person that I love freely and leave in peace. We will never do anything to harm or expose The Family, unlike my uncle whom his own father never trusted."

"Get rid of them," someone shouted.

"No!" Paul shouted. "If you plan on getting rid of anyone, don't kill Nell. She has nothing to do with any of this. If you want to take your anger and fears out on someone, just do it to me, but let her go."

There was an unnerving silence as members slowly lined next to each other, side by side, exposing the stairs to the cabin. Wally and Bill dragged both Paul and Nell into the cabin, followed by Harry who closed the door behind them. Bill pointed the barrel of his rifle to Paul's head.

"Shall we go ahead and shoot?" he asked.

"No," said Harry, coldly. "Shooting would be too good for the likes of *them*. You know what to do. Beat them! Beat them to death, starting with Paul!"

"Isn't that extreme?" Bill asked, eyeballing his father with surprising hesitation.

Wally leered wickedly. He lowered his rifle, chuckling unpleasantly.

"He *did* have your girl alone with him in the bathroom during the last get together," he said, smirking at Paul, as if savoring the moment.

"What are you trying to say, Wally?" Bill demanded, lowering his own rifle, and tilting his head to the side questionably.

"I'm saying this," Wally said, nonchalantly. "Why show mercy to someone who your girl slept with not too long ago? You know that if he is still alive, she will always go back running to him. He did take her before and is capable of doing it again."

Bill turned red with rage and confronted Paul shaking with fury. Bill's nostrils became flared, and his breathing became rapid. He angrily put his rifle to the ground and began to crack his knuckles. His bulging eyes zoned onto Paul as he bared his teeth.

"That's not true," Paul bellowed. "Nothing happened in the bathroom with Nancy that day!"

Bill struck a forceful blow to Paul's head. Paul fell to the floor, unconscious. Nell's mouth fell open as she screamed in horror. She attempted to push herself towards her fallen boyfriend, but Wally grabbed her by the back of her shirt, yanking her away. Full of fury, Bill raised his fist to deliver another deadly blow.

Boom!

Bill shrieked in agony, grabbing his now blooded hand. Harry, Wally, and Nell froze, unsure of what just happened. They turned to the door of a room that open and the barrel of a rifle pointing at Bill. Someone else was in the cabin with them! Harry took his rifle and began to fire into the room that had the stranger.

Boom! Boom!

"Finish him off, you dumbass," Harry shouted at Bill, still firing into the other room. Bill disregarded his father, focusing more on his injured hand that now had a hole in it and was bleeding.

Boom!

Suddenly, Harry screamed in pain himself, dropping his rifle. His own shoulder was now blooded. He shouted as another bullet zoomed towards him, hitting his leg. Harry fell to the floor. He reached for his rifle again as Wally began to fire into the room. Unexpectedly, Wally's rifle jammed, causing him to panic. He reached for Bill's fallen rifle, but a bullet zoomed between him and the fallen rifle, forcing him back. Harry reached for his weapon but was shot in the hand. Harry howled in anguish as a red-haired young man stepped further out the room. It was Henry.

"You bastards do anything else to Paul and I will kill every last one of you," Henry said.

"You're that Wilkerson kid," Harry shouted. "You better shoot me dead because you're good as gone if you don't!"

"I definitely can make that happen," Henry said lifting his rifle. Harry's eyes widened, turning to Wally.

"Shoot him, you idiot!" Harry shouted at Wally.

"It's jammed," Wally yelled, struggling.

"Do and you'll be next to be shot," Henry said to Wally. "Lower the rifle and slowly back away from it or I'll blast you out of this cabin!"

Wally lowered the rifle to the ground and backed away from it. Henry stepped closer to Bill and Harry's rifles and kicked them away from the father and son. Henry eyed Bill and Harry.

"You two, in against the wall," Henry ordered. Bill and Harry slowly scooted by the wall. Henry looked at Nell, some reluctance in his eyes. "You, pick up one of those rifles and shoot them if they try anything." He waited as Nell grabbed Bill's rifle, shaking. Henry, then, looked at his unconscious friend that lay on the floor and groaned. Henry refocused his glance on Wally. "You are going to send everyone away or I will blow your head off." He nodded towards the door, forcing Wally to head to the entrance of the cabin.

Shaking, Nell glanced at Paul's still unconscious body. She heard cheering, the sounds of people scurrying, and cars starting. Shortly, Henry and Wally reemerged with Henry still holding his rifle to Wally's back. With a forceful blow, Henry struck Wally in the back of the head with the stock of his rifle. Wally cried out before falling unconscious to the ground.

"My fucking hand," Bill cried out, still clutching his hand.

"You're lucky that's all I shot," Henry exclaimed, now peeking out the window. People were still chattering outside, annoying him. Swiftly, Henry began to disarm all the rifles except for his. Once he was finished, Henry peered outside the window again and saw the lights to the last car driving away. Once more, Henry struck Harry with the stock of his rifle, knocking him out cold. Henry placed his rifle on the ground and approached Bill.

"This is for Paul, you son of a bitch," He balled his fist and struck Bill to the ground, knocking him out as well. Henry retrieved his rifle and with his free arm, Henry grabbed ahold of Paul's arm and lifted him off the ground. Nell quickly grabbed ahold of Paul as well and they both promptly exited the cabin. Henry helped pull Paul to his vehicle. He hurried to the front seat while Nell got into the back seat with Paul. Henry placed his rifle near the passenger side of his vehicle. He pressed his foot to the gas pedal and sped away with Paul and Nell into the darkness. The car swerved wildly down the road until they hit a familiar road. Henry slowed the car down, knowing that a few members of The Family that were part of the police force would be nearby. He forced himself to drive within the speed limit until they were out of town.

Henry looked back and forth between the backseat and the road, worried about Paul. He had been driving for an hour and they were no longer in Wood Oak. He gawked angrily at Nell as she continued to hold Paul in her arms with tears running down her face.

"This is all *your* fault," Henry spat at Nell. Slamming on the breaks, the car squealed as it came to a sudden halt. Henry parked the car to the side of the road and climbed out. He flung open the back door, grabbed Nell by the wrist, and dragged her out of the vehicle.

"Let me go," Nell shouted yanking at his hand before being hurled to the ground. Henry reached back into the front seat and grabbed his rifle. He pointed it at her.

"Get out of here," he said. "I better not ever see you again."

"Paul," Nell cried out, trying to crawl back towards the car. Henry fired a warning shot inches away from her. Nell quickly backed away. Her face was covered in tears and her knees were now scraped from the rocky surface of the ground.

"Don't you *ever* go near Paul ever again," Henry continued. "You ruined his life! I'd shoot you dead right now, if it weren't for him."

There was a muffled groan from the backseat of the car. Henry slammed the door shut. He put his rifle into the front seat and got back inside. Leaving Nell to the side of the road, Henry sped down the road. He peered through the rear-view mirror to see Paul's blooded head.

"Don't worry, buddy," Henry said. "I'm gonna take you to a hospital."

"Nell," Paul said faintly, "where is Nell?"

Henry ignored the question. Frantically, he searched for signs for nearby hospitals. They were in an unfamiliar area, frustrating Henry who banged his fists against the steering wheel.

"Henry," Paul said, "What happened? Where is Nell?"

"Will you shut up about her," Henry yelled, driving faster. Coming upon a slower car, Henry veered wildly to avoid hitting them. The person from the other car blew their horn. All of a sudden, Henry slammed on his breaks. The other driver jammed on his breaks and veered to the right to avoid crashing into Henry's car.

"Learn to drive, asshole," the other driver shouted, now driving past them.

"Fuck you," Henry shouted. He struck his fists against the steering wheel as he glanced at his wounded friend once again. He saw the streaks of tears that trailed from Paul's face, intermingling with the blood that wept from his head. Henry turned the car around, swearing more in the process. He drove a few yards back, stopped the car once again, and exited the vehicle. Paul soon heard screams and the backdoor to the car flew open. Henry shoved Nell back into the vehicle next to Paul.

"Nell," Paul said, touching her arm. Crying hysterically, Nell embraced Paul.

"Dammit, Paul," Henry said. "You're as good as dead, and for what, someone like *her*? This has got to be one of the stupidest things you've ever done!"

Paul smiled wrapping an arm around Nell.

"I'd do it again for someone like her," he said. "Believe it or not, it's one of the *best* things I've done."

Epilogue

Paul sat down next to Nell with Henry sitting directly across from them in the restaurant. Down to the last few dollars that they had between them, Paul caressed the back of Nell's hand with his thumb, out in the open. The waitress placed three plates of food out before them: bacon, eggs, and grits. Returning to Wood Oak would not be an option for any of them. Thus, losing any hopes of receiving any of the four university scholarships offered to Paul. Luckily, Henry had an aunt who lived an hour away on the outskirts of Florida. With a few coins in hand, Henry called her, and she informed them that they could stay with her for a while. Paul, the teen, who once had it all: popularity, lots of money, and everything most teens could possibly want, was now an outcast. Once he thought about it, all that he really wanted and needed were friends who truly cared about him. He embraced the support of his friend, Henry, and the love of his life, Nell. Paul looked out the window to the restaurant, his eyes landing on a recruiting station across the street for the United States Marine Corps. He smiled, taking a bite of his breakfast.

Made in the USA
Columbia, SC
30 May 2021